CROSBY'S CHALLENGE

BY

BECCA BEJARANO

Dedication

During the last year of my father's life, I was privileged to spend numerous hours enjoying his company. Many days, I would sit at the dining room table working on my book while he watched television. He would periodically ask me how my book was coming along. There were times when I would read him a chapter and ask him his opinion. He was always ready and willing to give me some honest feedback. During his last weeks with us, he and I were quietly talking about several things he had on his mind. That day he took my hand and made his last request of me. He asked me to promise him that I would finish writing my book and be sure to have it published. I silently cried, picked up his hand, and brought it to my lips as I kissed his hand while letting him know that I would follow this journey to the very end.

Acknowledgment

I would like to thank my husband for his continuous belief and encouragement throughout my journey in writing this book. I could not have done this without your support, my love. To my Children and Grandchildren, thank you for your belief in me throughout this entire process. Mia, thank you, my big girl, for the inspiration you pored through me in my thought process. Jennifer, my beautiful niece, thank you for your insightful input and your words of encouragement. To all of my family without you and the excitement you shared while I rambled on about my quest, I thank you! I love each and every one of you so much.

To Kay Harris, thank you for believing in me and trusting me as your Safe Home Director so many years ago. Because of this experience I met my muse for this book. I also met one of the most inspirational women who became my best friend during my time there. I love and miss you, Traci Patton.

Elle, your hard work editing for me. Your encouraging words warm my heart. You are so very special to me.

Amber, thank you for your hard work with the art. You did a beautiful job.

Contents

Chapter One

The Little Secret

When a child is born, it's not just their physical body that emerges; a unique soul is born as well. This child will develop their own personality, make their own choices, and create their own world. To them, this world may seem perfect, but their vision of perfection will inevitably be shaped by their surroundings, particularly the home they are nurtured in. Children develop their personalities by picking up traits from their surroundings, often mirroring their parents. They may inherit certain characteristics from their father and others from their mother, resulting in a unique blend that brings a new personality into the world. Essentially, a child's personality can be seen as a combination of both parents' influences. As they grow, children imitate habits and behaviors they observe, whether it's a specific gesture or a particular way of speaking, viewing these as achievements in their own development.

Have you ever noticed how young children often struggle to fit into their parents' shoes? This playful act stems from their desire to feel grown-up. In their subconscious minds, parents are seen as supermodels and heroes, embodying the ideals they aspire to be one day; that's in their nature, and that's how they are going to make their world by taking their parents as inspirations.

When Crosby was born, her parents felt like the luckiest couple in the world. After three years of trying to conceive and facing numerous challenges, they were finally blessed with their daughter. For her mother, it was the most fortunate day of her life, a day filled with hope for their family. Crosby entered the world as a beam of joy for her parents. Her father brought chocolates for the whole hospital, and everybody was cheering on her birth as if all the sorrows of their life were now turned into blessings.

Today, Crosby is a wonderfully spirited 9-year-old four-foot petite little girl; her skin is a beautiful olive tone with rosy cheeks and warm hazel eyes. Crosby's hair is long brown and curly; she seldom wears it down and says it's best kept in a high ponytail; otherwise, it's all over the place. She often jokes, saying that birds will nest in all of her wild curls if she doesn't tame them.

When she looks at you with her warm hazel eyes and plump pink lips with just the right amount of a pout, there is not a soul that could bear to utter the word "no" to her. The family loved to make jokes about her puppy dog eyes and the power behind them. Her eyes are really attractive as if they have their own world in them, and anybody who sees them wants to be a part of that world. For a nine-year-old, Crosby is more intelligent than other children. She has something in it, something very unique, not common in every other nine-year-old. The way she manages herself and carries herself is something like a work of art. For someone new, Crosby would come across as a little older than usual, nine years. Her face is confident, and there is a certain determination in her eyes. She handles more than she can, let it be the household chores or helping her younger sister; Crosby is always one step ahead of her age. It seems like she wants everything to be perfect, and her only aim is to achieve excellence, and she enjoys getting there.

However, lately there is a mystery behind the smile that did not meet her eyes. We all know that *"Face is the index of mind,"* and from her face, one could see that something is definitely missing; her expressions are not the same as they used to be. Before, she was a bit carefree, but now she takes care of everything around her.

Being the eldest of two, she often felt as though she had to carry some form of happiness for both herself and her younger sister. From the very beginning, she has been deeply concerned about Hailey, wanting nothing more than for her world to be perfect. She strives to ensure that Hailey's life is filled with magic, doing everything she can to shield her from any catastrophe or even the slightest hint of any setback to her world.

Hailey is seven years old; she favors her mother's features. Hailey has pale skin, green eyes, and long, straight blonde hair. She loves to sing and dance all the time. For Crosby, this can sometimes get annoying; other times, you can catch the sisters singing into their hair brushes and dancing on their beds. She lets Crosby know constantly that she is her very best friend, and Crosby loves it...

Lately, Crosby has been struggling with her own little secret, which she chooses to hold on to, believing that if anyone broke through her truth, she would no longer be able to continue to conceal her secret. She chooses always to keep up the appearance of a happy-go-lucky child while inside her, she is facing turmoil, but she is not telling anyone. Above all, she is concerned about Hailey. She understands that as long as her secret remains safe, Hailey's perfect world is secure. However, if that secret were to be revealed, there's a real risk that Hailey's world could crumble before it even has a chance to take shape.

At first sight, one would see a vibrant, tenacious, and confident child. Her studious face is enough to give you an idea of how responsible Crosby is; there is something with her body language that resonates so perfectly with being the eldest child and taking up tasks and responsibilities. Her mannerism reflects that if she takes responsibility for something, that thing is surely taken care of. If it is your first time meeting her, there is no reason to question her happiness. Several years of hiding your feelings from your unhappy parents soon becomes an art, and Crosby is a wonderful artist. You would never know what's behind that smile, that laughter, or that smartly spoken sentence.

At first, she faced difficulty doing that, but by the time she mastered it and because she had to do it every day and every moment in front of Hailey so now, even she didn't know whether she was laughing or joking full-heartedly or just for the sake of Hailey's happiness. To her, she thinks that being an elder sister, it is her responsibility to maintain happiness for both of them and so far, she has been doing it without a single holiday; she has been acting each day. One can imagine how hard it is to look happy or laugh when all you want to do is just cry and let all your emotions out, but Crosby makes a difficult decision and chooses to smile anyway.

Chapter Two

School Days

Today, as Crosby is walking through the school hallways in a daze, confused by the energy that is flowing through her body, she feels as though she is just floating from classroom to classroom. She feels completely disconnected from her surroundings as if she were a robot without any inherent emotions to help her connect with the situations happening around her.

Well, this is not new to her; she has been dealing with the same kind of state for the past two years when she first saw her mother yelling at her father. She got to see a totally different side of her. Before that incident, to her, her mother was a kind, polite, and soft-hearted person, but that incident shook the foundation of her mother's persona to her. At first, she couldn't understand what had happened between her father and mother. Her mother was completely mad at her father, and she didn't even give him a chance to say anything. He quietly left the home without a word. His face was full of frustration; he saw Crosby in the hallway but didn't say a word. He picked up his keys, and the next thing Crosby heard was the engine roaring and then fading in the distance.

That night, she cried a lot in bed, and her pillow became soaked. In her innocent mind, she struggled to accept that her own mother could do this to her loving and caring father, who never let anything bad happen to his family.

This was her first bad experience with her mother, and since then, she hasn't been the same. Now, she sees her mother, screaming and yelling at her father about every minor and or a major thing. Sometimes, even their father also retaliates and speaks loudly, but she realizes that it is her mother who is instigating the matter every time. This all leads to an extremely uncomfortable environment at home, and Crosby feels it. This horrible feeling penetrates her personality, and now, when she sees her father and mother even just talking, she feels scared that this situation may escalate and lead to a horrible fight.

The following day at school, she found herself trapped in the same emotional state she had experienced at home. So, for Crosby, this was now normal, and she had found a way to deal with this; she just let it happen. She doesn't do anything to come out of this state because she knows that this will happen again so there is no point in fighting with this thing again and again. From that day till date, she has created a protective shield around her and she has been carrying that burden ever since. Though her tiny shoulders are not strong enough to carry such weight, still, she is doing it, but deep inside her, she has even accepted this as the fate of her home.

Her mother's bad treatment of her father is the main cause that often leads to her conflicts with her father. Although her father tries very hard to be polite and gentle at times even, he retaliates a little bit. This is her mother, who every time manages to find the fault and start a conflict. Sometimes, the conflict goes on for more than a week, and her mother constantly throws sarcasm and mean comments at her father.

For Crosby, the school is her getaway. At least, for a few hours, she can be that little nine-year-old girl that she is because, at home, she is not just a nine-year-old. Crosby is Hailey's big sister, and their mom says she needs to be a good role model for Hailey. This means she has to follow all the rules their mom sets. Sometimes, Crosby wishes she didn't have to be an older sister and thinks about how nice it would be if she didn't have one. But then she remembers that's not how things are nor would she want to change them. She knows that she would never be happy without her little sister.

However, to deal with this, Crosby found a little trick at school; when she is on the playground, she just hits the ground running. This helps her to expel all the negative energy that she carries from her home.

Chapter Three

Ms. Traci

Ms. Traci is her literature teacher and favorite by far. Crosby loves her enthusiastic form of teaching and compassion for her students. She is tall and slender with green eyes that change color with her moods. She has shoulder-length, straight, dirty blonde hair. Her skin color is lightly tanned, her smile radiates through her classroom with warmth and charm, and her students crave her excitement and animation as she delivers her book readings. The students in her classroom adore her for her unmatched care and attentiveness. Her thoughtful approach to teaching and nurturing them creates a supportive environment that they truly appreciate, and on weekends, they crave weekdays so that they will meet their best teacher in the school. How innocent are the admirations and inspirations of childhood. They create such a beautifully enchanting world for the children that the kids never want to leave it. Even as adults, people long for and reminisce about their school days, cherishing those simple, innocent dreams. Many believe that the best part of their lives was spent in that nurturing environment.

In Crosby's opinion, Ms. Traci is by far the best teacher at her school. Teaching is her passion, but more than that, she simply wants to be with kids. All she seeks is to give them the attention and care they deserve, and that's why she is everybody's favorite.

Ms. Traci does not have any children of her own yet, she considers her students as her own. Therefore, they are treated with extra love and compassion. When her students have problems outside of schoolwork, she makes herself available to them when they come to her for assistance. No matter how busy the schedule is, she always makes time for her students, reflecting her true caring nature.

She also makes it a point to let the children know that she is available to help them with questions they may have in other subjects. This allows her to reach out to the other teachers as they work together for the kid's sake.

She started an afternoon gathering with her peers to compare notes on the student's academic needs. The students are attracted to her because of her friendliness and approachable demeanor. She is kind and caring, indeed the true qualities of a teacher. She has also taught and encouraged her students to respect each other and never shy away from showing compassion and respect to one another.

The classroom is set up differently than most classrooms due to Ms. Traci's eccentric taste and desire to create a unique environment for her students. Ms. Traci spoke with the principal about searching for furniture and different items to be able to decorate her classroom and make it inviting for her students.

She went to an estate sale outside of the city in a small town in the area and found antique student desks; the owner explained to her that he was planning on taking the desks to the dump. She offered to purchase them at her own expense and explained her need for the desks; he just said, "Lady, those are ready for the dump, but you can have them if you think you can use them."

She painted them pastel green with random streaks, each with the left side top corner painted with chalkboard paint so that her students could write their names on their desks; this allowed for the class exchange as the day moved forward.

She painted an entire wall with chalkboard paint so that her students would have a place to express themself; she provided several buckets of chalk with every color of chalk imaginable. Another wall was decorated with an array of emoji faces; sometimes, the students would place sticky notes on the faces that best described their emotions for that day. She had a wall that had a mural of a unique woodland area with beautiful flowers, birds, and benches to create a serene atmosphere.

On the floor she placed different size and colored bean bags for the students. Her goal was to always give the students a comfortable place of retreat throughout the day.

After her classes ended, she would take a moment to explore the walls of the classroom, where students had left notes and messages. Each note would offer her a chance to look deeply into their thoughts and struggles, helping her gain a better understanding of their experiences in her class and also in general.

As she reads through their notes, she feels a connection to their journeys, and it inspires her to alter her approach to better meet their needs. This practice has helped change her classroom into a space of shared learning where every voice matters.

This also gives her the opportunity to discover problems the students might express on the board or chosen faces. Sometimes, children would place wish I was here stickers on the woodland wall. Through this method, she gets to know where the aspirations of her students are headed and what and where they want to be in life. And after getting to know them better, she guides them and helps them in achieving their goals.

She embraces the seriousness of the information and takes it to heart in hopes of helping her students if they choose to come to her. If they choose not to come to her, she would research books that would gently provide a sort of scenario with insight into the problem they were experiencing.

Singling a child out has never been her style. She chooses this form of teaching because this allows the students a way to easily come out of their dilemmas.

Yesterday afternoon, Crosby had drawn a simple round face; however, rather than being a happy face, it was a frown in the middle of a garden full of thorns. This got her attention in a way that not even a book she could research would help. She knew that she was going to need a special kind of help for Crosby.

Chapter Four

Shifting

As Crosby entered the classroom today, she could not help but feel the shift in the atmosphere. When she was taking each step toward her desk, she felt tingles in her body. Every step she took intensified the tingling that consumed her body. As she sat in her chair, she felt a new sensation in her body that was beyond her comprehension. For a change, Crosby did not feel any fear; she felt a sense of relief and excitement.

As she was sitting in her chair, she noticed that there was a girl who looked exactly like her standing by the window, watching her every move. She realized that it wasn't just any girl. She was watching her own self. She then wondered, "Am I dead?" But no, she did not feel despair or fear. How could this be possible? What was happening? How on earth am I watching myself and not gasping for air? She wondered, has anyone else noticed that I am sitting in this chair and standing by the window? Did someone put me in a sci-fi movie and not mention it to me? Crosby thought about letting Ms. Traci know what she was experiencing, but would she think that she was going crazy? This thought stopped her from sharing this new experience with her favorite teacher.

Crosby often had a problem sharing her feelings, so when she drew the face on the wall, it was something out of her normal being, and she felt a strange emotional release, a way to express what couldn't be said easily. Even before the divorce of her parents, she had issues talking about her feelings. Now, it feels nearly impossible; the divorce has only made her turn more into herself and keep her feelings bottled up. The divorce just compelled her to tighten the walls around her heart. When asked how she is doing, she will respond with a smile and say that she is fine, masking the chaos she is dealing with herself.

As Crosby stood at the window watching herself, she noticed the sadness in her eyes that was not visible to anyone else. It was a heavyweight for just a nine-year-old; feels like there was a scream that was trapped within her. She quickly wiped away the stray tear that dared to stream down her cheek. She was sitting in the chair remembering yesterday's events before she left for school, how her mother was wildly screaming at her father and calling him names. Her body cringed into itself at the memory. She felt a cold wave around her, which pushed her into discomfort.

Chapter Five

Family

Crosby sat quietly, listening to her mother, who was on the phone with someone speaking in a very sarcastic manner. She knew that this tone of voice and sarcasm was spoken only when her mother was speaking to her father. She has been listening to it since she was 7 years old. This sent her stomach into summersaults every time. It just never got any easier. Sometimes, she would think back to happier memories of their family that felt whole, but those are now there only to be crushed by her reality.

Crosby loves her parents deeply, and although she cannot help being angry with her mother at this moment, her father repeatedly expresses to her that she should always love and respect her mom; no matter what happens, she will always be her mother and would love her. But how can she, when she understands that her mother has left her father for another man? She never even worried about anyone else's feelings in the matter. Crosby felt hurt and betrayed by her mother, and she often wondered why her parents didn't try harder to keep the family together.

Jason is a good man, and he cares for her and her sister but he just is not her father, and Crosby wants her mother to remember this fact. Sometimes, she feels bad because Jason sometimes looks rather sad; she wonders what it is that makes him sad. She has never asked him because she does not want him to know that she cares; this would probably give him the idea that she is okay with the situation. She is not.

Crosby is expected to share the same kind of love that she has for her father with Jason. For Crosby, this task is near impossible; to her just nine-year-old brain, this whole situation is incomprehensible, while on the other hand, her mother just cannot seem to understand that her father is their life. Gabriel and Maya were wonderful parents until Maya met Jason, she thinks to herself.

Gabriel is a handsome man; he is of average height, although moderately muscular, with dark brown hair, hazel eyes, and olive-colored skin. His favorite thing to do with his family is to cuddle on the couch and watch movies. He also enjoys taking the family on outings to the museums and art galleries. Maya is a petite woman with fair skin, light brown hair, and sky-blue eyes. She enjoys hiking, Jogging and playing in the park with her daughters. Crosby favors her father in appearance yet has her mother's personality, while Hailey favors her mother in appearance; she favors her father's personality. They always said that they were a perfect family in regard to their genes. They never thought about having any more children because they felt blessed with each having a child that resembled each of them.

Then, Jason came into the picture. He is her mother's boyfriend. He is tall and muscular and has pale skin, blonde hair, and green eyes. He is very gentle and generous with complements for the girls and their mother. He is funny and full of life; however, she will not admit that to him. To Crosby, doing so felt like betraying her dad.

As her mother's relationship with her boyfriend grew stronger, her mother's ability to make Crosby's dad feel worse grew as well. Her father has always been practical yet loving, her dad and Jason are opposite in personality.

Crosby couldn't understand why her mother didn't see how much her dad was hurting. Even though her father kept telling her to respect her mother, Crosby felt torn between love and the pain of seeing her family fall apart.

Chapter Six

The Day Before

For an extended period of time, her father seemed distant and withdrawn, but her mother never missed the opportunity to degrade him in front of the children. Crosby hated watching her mother degrading her father. She couldn't understand why her mother treated him this way, especially since, in Crosby's eyes, it was her mother who had broken the family apart. She wonders why they don't just get along with each other and remember the love that the family used to share.

Today was no different. Somehow, her mother's sarcasm was worse than usual. Crosby knew that her mother was not aware of her standing quietly next to the wall that separated the kitchen and living room, listening to her mother scream at her father yet again. Sometimes, she felt like her mother was attempting to tone down her voice while the children were around, but not this time. She didn't seem to care how loud she was.

And once again Crosby's day was filled with more despair than she expected. Sometimes, she even thinks to stop hoping for something better because it is not happening at all. Well, for today, all her father wanted was to be able to pick his daughters up after school for a chance to celebrate Crosby's birthday. Her mother was very quick to remind him that he has a scheduled time to visit with his daughters, and today was not that day. There was no way she would ever allow her father any extra time, no matter how often he tried. Crosby secretly wishes that one day her mother would realize how much she and her sister missed their dad, but again, she thinks that day will never come because her mother is getting bitter with her dad even more.

Deciding to step into the moment, Crosby made her presence known, careful not to let on that she had overheard the entire conversation. Crosby proceeded to address her mom, "Mom, is dad coming to my birthday party tonight?"

"No," her mother said, "You will see him next weekend as usual," her tone was as strict as always.

"But today is my birthday. Can I at least see him today?" Crosby requested; her eyes were almost filled with tears.

"Crosby, you are giving me a headache. Can you just please go get ready for school without any extra problems?" Her mother completely ignored the innocent request and gave her the orders. Crosby hung her head and sighed since she knew there was no reasoning with her mother.

Chapter Seven

Journey Begins

As Crosby sat at her desk, something felt different. She noticed she was no longer standing by the window. Confused, she looked back and forth to make sure she wasn't imagining things. Then, she looked towards the front of the classroom and realized that there was a beautiful large door with delicate carvings of differently shaped flowers that she had never seen in her life.

Her eyes widened in amazement. How could this be? It was just a regular closet before. She looked around the classroom, watching her classmates to see if they noticed the door as well. When no one looked as though they saw the difference in the door, she decided that this experience was meant only for her.

Suddenly, she felt as though she was being carried towards the door; the excitement in her body grew as she came closer to the door. The doorknob was a beautiful bronze color with deep indentations and curves with each creating a unique pattern she did not recognize. As she reached for the knob, she felt a bubbly sensation in her stomach, and her breath hitched with excitement. Her eyes were filled with sparks and shined so that the gold specks in them increased to a new level. She was excited and scared all at once, but for the first time in six months, she felt a real, honest smile spread across her face.

She didn't understand why this was making her so happy; she only knew that she felt something strange and wonderful. She knew that something extraordinary was about to happen. She couldn't even explain it to herself, but it was like a promise of magic and adventure waiting just beyond that door.

With a mixture of excitement and nerves, she turned the knob and stepped through, her heart racing as she wondered what she would find on the other side. As she crossed the threshold, her eyes widened at the sight before her. It was grand—more beautiful and awe-inspiring than anything she had ever seen. She blinked and rubbed her eyes, trying to make sense of it all, whispering to herself, *Why me?*

From across the classroom, Ms. Traci watched silently, a small, knowing smile tugging at the corners of her lips. She stood behind one of the student's desks, her hand gripping the back of the chair as she held her breath. Ms. Traci knew exactly what was waiting for Crosby. She could feel the emotion building inside her because she knew this was going to be the most wonderful, magical moment of Crosby's life. And she was ready to witness it.

Chapter Eight

Meeting Hansen

Beyond the door was a spectacular garden larger and more beautiful than she had ever seen. In the center of the garden was a lovely bench covered with intricate carvings and surrounded by extraordinary birds that fluttered about, their feathers shimmering like gems. Next to the bench was an unusual golden perch for the most exotic bird she had ever laid eyes on. The perch was unusually low with the most intricate designs that she had ever seen.

Crosby felt a magnetic pull towards the bench and gently sat next to the exotic bird that was perched on the beautiful bench. She was startled and nearly jumped out of her skin when the bird simply said, "Hello, Crosby, I've been waiting for you."

In a state of shock, she exclaimed, "Wait, you can talk, and you know my name? And what do you mean that you have been waiting for me?" Her voice was filled with excitement.

"You, my dear Crosby, have been chosen by our high commander to complete the ultimate challenge." The bird calmly replied.

Her mind raced with questions. "Who is your high commander she asked, and what kind of challenge are you talking about?"

The bird tilted his head, eyes gleaming, "This information is not of importance to you at this moment; we just need to begin our journey."

"Wait!" Crosby interrupted, panic started to build up in her, "I'm on a journey? What about school and my family, and how long am I going to be gone? How can you expect me to run around here without any information at all?"

The bird's voice softened. "Please do not concern yourself with that at this moment. This journey is special and will not interfere with your family and school. You are in a safe environment; the high commander would never put you in harm's way."

The bird nodded gently, "Shall we go?"

"No, wait," Crosby hesitated. "Can you at least tell me your name because I'm not supposed to talk to strangers, and you are a stranger to me, even though you are a talking bird?"

The bird chuckled, "Oh, how simply rude of me. My name is Hansen, and since you are in a magical kingdom, I am not a stranger to you anymore."

Hansen was the most beautiful bird she had ever seen. He was tall with different shades of wonderous shiny grey feathers. His dark grey beak was molded with a broad front and flowed into a sleek, slender point as it formed the tip. His forehead was an insatiable black velvet oval shape, the tip of it high and regal; his cheekbones were a brilliant white, and, at the top point where these two colors met, they were separated with a crimson blood-red patch on either side of his cheekbones. He wore a shiny golden spray that resembled a unique crown, the tips of the spikes changing colors every few seconds as his head gently moved to be in her direct site.

"Shall we move forward?" Hansen asked again.

As she stared at him in grand amazement, she simply replied, "We shall," and lifted herself onto her feet. To her surprise, when Hansen stood to his feet, she realized he was eight feet tall.

Hansen lowered his head to her level and asked, "Are you okay?"

Her voice filled with wonder, she replied, "This challenge keeps getting increasingly tricky by every minute."

"How so? Hansen tilted his head.

"Well, to my surprise, I did not expect to be traveling through a beautiful garden with an 8-foot talking bird when I woke up this morning," Crosby replied.

Hansen chuckled warmly, "Hold on, sweet girl, the journey has only just begun."

She smiled at him and said, "This definitely beats going to school any old day! Let's move forward!"

Chapter Nine

Curiosity Peaked

She and Hansen began their journey through the beautiful garden in a peaceful silence. Crosby was pensive in her thoughts; Hansen simply watched as he could tell that she was in deep thoughts. The gentle rustling of leaves and the soft chirping of birds filled the air, but neither of them spoke, the serenity of the garden mirroring Crosby's inward reflection.

Finally, she spoke, "Hansen?" She asked with a timid voice, "While I am going to take this journey, will my family know that I am gone, and will they miss me and worry about me?" Her voice was filled with concern.

Hansen replied gently, "Sweetheart, unbelievably, time is standing still in your world as we travel through this magical world. If you glance into my eyes, you will see yourself sitting in your classroom with Ms. Traci."

Crosby was amazed at how she could watch herself in the eyes of this marvelous bird. "When you feel as though you are questioning your world's actions, please feel free to look into my eyes," Hansen continued, "I am here to make this journey as comfortable as possible for you.

He paused, then said kindly, "I would like to ask that you please take this opportunity to focus on your needs rather than your families. Focusing on yourself now will yield a better tomorrow for your entire family."

Crosby sighed, nodding slowly, "I will try, Hansen; taking care of my family has become as necessary as breathing for me lately. Before we move further, may I please check in on my sister? I worry about her; she's younger than me, and sometimes I find her crying for no reason at all."

Hansen smiled softly, "Yes, you may check in on your sister; remember, just look into my eyes."

Crosby peered into Hansen's eyes and saw her sister, Hailey, playing happily on the playground with her friends. A wave of relief washed over her.

Hailey has struggled with her parent's divorce, and her way of handling it has simply been avoidance. As the youngest child, she was shielded from most of the drama between her parents. Crosby made sure to protect her from as much drama as she could. She found herself playing upstairs with her doll house many times while Crosby would sit quietly at the top of the stairs, listening to her parents argue.

Seeing her sister safe and carefree, Crosby felt a little lighter. She looked up at Hansen, her heart still heavy but grateful for the moment of peace.

Chapter Ten

Loving Arms

As they were walking through the garden Crosby took notice of the sky and the sun. The sky was a magnificent shade of blue with wonderous touches of teal and gray fusing together and stretching into thin lines as they met the sun. The sky appeared to be touching the ground as if to coddle the blades of forest green and lime grass.

The sun, large and radiant, shone with beautiful shades of yellow and gold. Its warm rays seemed to tenderly embrace the vibrant, exotic flowers as if softly kissing their petals. Somehow, Crosby could feel the love that was being generated in the garden. It was as if the sun was caring for each flower like a young toddler in its mother's gentle arms. Crosby's mind went back to the days when she felt that kind of love from her mother. A wave of sadness crept into her heart as she wondered if she would ever feel that kind of warmth again.

The simplicity of her life had endured a drastic change; what felt like only a second had gradually happened within a matter of 3 years. Everything in her life changed the day her mom met Jason. Crosby couldn't understand how her mother could be so selfish, so focused on her own happiness without thinking about how it was affecting her and her younger sister.

In her mind, she wonders, isn't it true that parents are supposed to put their children's feelings and safety first? Crosby wants her mother to be happy, she just wishes that it did not have to be at the expense of her and her sister. She never felt unsafe in her home or around Jason. But she now feels like an intruder. She aches for the day when she will feel the warmth, love, and joy she used to feel in her home. The days when her family used to cuddle up on the couch, enjoy a good movie, and share a bowl of popcorn.

Breaking the silence, Hansen spoke softly, "I can sense your fears, Crosby."

Amazed, she asked, "You can read my mind as well? Please tell me is there anything you cannot do?"

"Oh, Crosby, just know that I am here to help you navigate through this magical world. Anything that is important to you is important to our High Commander, so my abilities are simply to benefit you," he chuckled again gently.

"Is it still too soon to ask who the High Commander is?" She asked with a hint of frustration.

Hansen smiled, his voice calm and patient, "My child, you are concerning yourself with things that will soon be revealed; there is no need to harp on things you cannot change."

"You know that as a child, my curiosity is mostly going to overpower my mind," Crosby sighed.

"Oh, I am very well aware of that fact, my dear; I just was optimistic about the fact that you might surprise me," Hansen replied with a wink.

"I promise to try and minimize my curiosity the best I can. However, I am still a child." Crosby said, smiling.

"That sounds great however, I would like for you to keep an open mind while traveling through my world," Hansen replied kindly.

"My mind is open; I am talking to a giant bird, after all; how much more open can I be," she said with a grin.

"No need for sarcasm, my dear; let's keep it light, please." Hansen raised an eyebrow.

"I am sorry, Hansen; I like you, so I will be better for you." Crosby giggled.

"Thank you, Crosby, that is greatly appreciated," Hansen said with a soft smile.

Chapter Eleven

Following the Florets

Hansen and Crosby continued through the garden, enjoying a lighthearted conversation; as they were walking up and down some small hills, Crosby noticed that the atmosphere was changing a little more each time they passed each hill. She began to see dandelion florets floating gently in the air, creating a magical scene that almost looked like snow.

"Hansen," she said, gazing at the delicate florets swirling around them, "This is a beautiful area, there are so many florets floating in the air it almost looks like it is snowing. Is someone blowing the florets into the air?"

Hansen smiled warmly, "No honey, we are getting closer to the area where you will be meeting Sedro."

"Whose Sedro, and why am I going to meet him, and what does he have to do with the florets?" Crosby asked, her curiosity piqued.

"Sedro is someone that will be asking you some particularly important questions," Hansen explained.

"I am not sure I like the sound of that," she replied with a concerned tone.

"It will be fine; the questions he will ask will only help you out on your journey. As far as the florets go, that is something you will have to see with your own eyes," Hansen explained again.

As they continued to travel on this path, Crosby began to realize that the flowers were growing larger.

"Hansen," she said, "These flowers bear a certain resemblance to a sunflower; however, there is something different about them."

He chuckled softly, "My sweet child, everything is different in my world; remember who you are traveling with."

Crosby and Hansen continued to walk the designated path; she continued to see the florets in the air; the more they walked towards the meadow, the thicker the florets began to gather. Crosby looked up at Hansen with a look of confusion on her face.

"What seems to be the problem, Crosby," Hansen asked.

"Can you hear that? Is someone singing?" She whispered.

"Oh, it must be Sedro; he believes that the world of Broadway will forever be at a loss since they will never get the chance to enjoy his beautiful voice." Hansen's eyes sparkled.

"Well, he does have a very lovely voice; I wonder, do you think that he will sing a song for me," Crosby giggled.

"We will need to tend to business first then you can ask him. Sedro never gives up the opportunity to sing to an audience, so your chances are grand." Hansen smiled.

"How does he even know about Broadway shows since he lives in the magical kingdom?" Crosby's eyes widened with excitement.

"Our world is magical; however, we are very connected to your world and its numerous entertainment methods," Hansen explained. "If you recall, I told you that you can see into your world through my eyes. My friends can do the same when their curiosity is at their highest peak."

"What about you? How can you see into my world?" Cosby asked.

"Never you mind, my child; all things will be revealed in due time." Hansen winked again.

Crosby sighed, but a smile crept onto her face. She was learning that in this magical world, every step of the journey held a mystery waiting to unfold.

Chapter Twelve

Meeting Sedro

Crosby caught her breath as warmth invaded her face, the vision that arose with the multitude of exotic flowers dancing to the song that was in the air. In the center of this vibrant display was an enormous wildflower, and Crosby knew instantly that it had to be Sedro.

Sedro was a mixture of a sunflower and a dandelion. His torso was a large stem with vibrant green and silver stripes, brown thorns, and a fuzzy surface. His head was a large yellow sunflower, his eyes were a brilliant malachite deep green, like the gem, and he had a dandelion floret as a nose with tiny speckles of silver.

As he sang, delicate florets floated from his mouth, drifting through the soft blush of the blue sky. They shimmered as the silver speckles sparkled in the sunlight. Sedro was the most beautiful singing flower Crosby had ever seen—and in truth, he was the only singing flower she had ever encountered. Surrounding him were smaller versions of himself, along with many other colorful flowers, all swaying gently in time with his lovely melody.

As Crosby and Hansen approached Sedro, his singing got louder and louder, yet his pitch was right on target. His voice was mezzo-soprano, which is between soprano and contralto; this made it mesmerizing at best. Before Sedro noticed that he had company, Crosby took the precious moment to soak up the beauty of his voice and appearance.

She couldn't help but think that she might never have the chance to witness such splendor again. In her world, her father had introduced her to many beautiful things, but nothing compared to the extraordinary beauty in front of her.

"Hansen, what brings you to this part of the garden?" Sedro asked, lilting with curiosity. "You seldom visit, and who do we have here?"

"Sedro, this is..."

"Crosby," Sedro finished Hansen's sentence with a playful roll of his eyes.

"Sedro, why do you ask such a question if you already know the answer," Hansen replied a hint of exasperation in his tone.

"Oh, it is much more fun to get you all fluster and see your eyes get all squinty and bitty," Sedro smirked, enjoying the playful banter.

"Well, you know that Crosby is here on her journey, and you are her next encounter," Hansen said.

"I am aware, my dear friend," Sedro replied with a nod, his eyes sparkling with mischief and delight.

Crosby stood before them, filled with anticipation, ready to embrace whatever wonders lay ahead in her journey with these extraordinary beings. Her heart raced as she looked at the bright colors and smelled the sweet flowers around her. The air felt alive, and the beautiful song from Sedro seemed to invite her into a world where anything could happen. A warm breeze brushed against her face, encouraging her to move forward. With each moment, she felt more connected to this magical place and the wonderful creatures there, eager to find out what fun adventures awaited her.

Chapter Thirteen

Questions Begin

Sedro turned his whole body to face Crosby as he spoke to her. "Crosby, do you understand why I am your second encounter?"

"Well," Crosby replied, "Hansen has told me that you will be asking me some important questions. I must be honest; however, I am a little intimidated and nervous because I don't really know why you would be asking these questions."

In a soft voice, Sedro replied, "You are on this journey because you have lost something very important, and you will have several encounters to help you find this lost gift. Shall we begin with the questions?"

"Wow! You just get right down to business, just like Hansen. Do you think maybe we could get to know each other first?" Crosby replied in a gentle tone.

"Oh, Crosby," Sedro responded, "We take our business to heart because we know how important it is for you in this journey, and we all want you to succeed."

He continued, "I will be asking you these questions; you may not know the answers, but carrying them with you throughout your journey will give you a better understanding and clarification in claiming your gift."

"Okay, I am ready for my questions, Sedro," Crosby said with a shy smile, squinting her eyes a bit.

"Very well, let us begin with the first question now. Crosby, do you know what might have caused you to lose your smile?" His voice was as calming as before.

"I smile all the time Sedro; people always give me different nicknames like smiley, smiles, chipper, and a few others. How can you say that I have lost my smile?" Crosby replied in a bit defensive manner.

"One can always see your smile, but can they feel your smile, Crosby?" Sedro asked in an intriguing manner.

"How can someone feel my smile, Sedro?" Crosby replied.

"When your smile can make one feel warmth and a near embrace, only then can one feel the truth of your smile," Sedro said, highlighting the difference.

"Crosby, can you tell me where a true smile is born?" He asked another question.

"Sedro, how can a smile be born? Is this even possible?" Crosby replied; she was confused.

"Crosby, your smile is born from your heart; only then can it truly be real. All our feelings stem from the heart; as we feel and share our true emotions, we can convey what is in our hearts." Sedro explained to her in a polite tone.

"Are you saying that my heart is not working? Does my smile need to be reborn? And if this must happen, how can it happen?" Crosby asked innocently.

"Crosby, as you continue in your journey, your heart will mend, and it will be stronger than ever before," Sedro reassured her.

"Crosby, while you were in the classroom, you drew a smiley face surrounded by thorns. Can you tell me what you were feeling when you surrounded the face with thorns?" Sedro added another question to the conversation.

Crosby's body stiffened, and a slight frown was visible on her face. "I was feeling trapped and like something was poking my body with a million toothpicks. I felt like if I took a breath, I was going to lose all the air in my body." Crosby explained her feelings.

"Crosby, can you remember what you were thinking while you were drawing this picture?" Sedro continued with questions.

Crosby took a moment before responding to think back to the events of the morning before the drawing, and then she replied, "My mother was screaming at my dad again over the phone. It was like she was meaner than she has ever been to my dad." Her tone was vividly shaky towards the end.

"I just want to know why she hates him so much and why my sister and I are being kept from him," Crosby asked with all her innocence.

"Crosby, your heart is breaking for you, your sister, and your father; as we travel in your journey, we will begin to unravel your emotions, and you will find the answers you are looking for," Sedro responded. His tone was encouraging.

"Sedro, can you give me any other insight on the thorns? I don't understand; I thought that you would give me a better answer." Crosby replied.

"Sometimes the answers to these questions are harder for us to receive, so we must be patient for the perfect time to hear and accept the answers," Sedro replied with his charming and relaxing tone.

"So, you're saying that I'm not ready to know the answer," said Crosby; she was evidently a little impatient at this point.

"That is correct, Crosby; as you travel through the kingdom, you will encounter someone who will be able to enlighten you, help you find the answer, and teach you how to accept it." Once again, Sedro encouraged her to believe in the process of the journey and that she would get all her answers.

Crosby stared at Sedro for a long moment, contemplating what he had just told her. After a while, she simply gave him a weak smile and shrugged her shoulders as if accepting the path ahead. Although she didn't receive all of the answers she felt she needed, she felt a slight calmness in her mind that allowed her to continue on her journey.

Chapter Fourteen

Singing with Sedro

Crosby reminded Sedro of her desire to sing a song with him. Sedro was elated at the idea; he disbursed a vast number of florets through the air in his glee. Crosby giggled at the site of the florets and asked, "What should we sing?" She asked with a grin, bouncing on her toes.

Sedro furrows his malachite eyes to search his mind for the perfect song. Crosby jumped up and down excitedly when Sedro shared with her the song they would sing. Crosby's eyes sparkled, and she clapped her hands with excitement. They began to sing the song, realizing that they were in perfect harmony.

"You are my sunshine, my only sunshine,

You make me happy when the skies are gray,

You will never know just how much I love you,

Please don't take my sunshine away."

As they sang, Sedro swayed gently, and Crosby joined him, both moving to the melody.

Then, Sedro suggested another song, and they sang, voices bright and full.

"Sing a rainbow, sing along with me.

Red and yellow and pink and green,

Purple and orange and blue.

I can sing a rainbow, sing a rainbow, sing a rainbow too!

Listen with your eyes, listen with your eyes,

And sing everything you see,

You can sing a rainbow, sing a rainbow, sing along with me."

Crosby was so happy singing with Sedro that they continued to sing a few more songs. Crosby's laughter filled the meadow. They then sang *Michael Row the Boat Ashore, Wheels on the Bus, Bingo,* and several others. She twirled around in delight, her voice and Sedro's mingling in the warm, flower-filled air.

Just then, Hansen cut in and announced that they had to continue their journey.

"Hansen, can we please stay a little longer? I'm having so much fun with Sedro." Crosby asked.

With a gentle smile on his face, he said, "I'm sorry, but we still have a long journey ahead of us." Hansen shook his head gently, resting a hand on Crosby's shoulder, and continued, "The purpose of your journey is not about having fun with Sedro; he has a way of making you forget the real reason for your journey. I'm very happy that he has helped you to release some of your true happiness, but this is only the beginning of your journey. You will meet others, and it is possible that you will have the same reaction; I will have to count on you to stay focused on the task at hand."

Crosby nodded slowly, looking at Hansen with understanding. "You're right, Hansen," she murmured. She turned back to Sedro, her expression softening as she took a step forward.

As they prepared to move forward on their journey, Sedro spoke out to Crosby. "Crosby, please remember that you must accept your truths no matter how difficult the dilemma is to change the circumstances in your life." He spoke gently, his voice warm and kind.

"Thank you, Sedro. I shall do my best." Crosby went up to Sedro and hugged his tall, fuzzy torso tightly. She let a little sniffle escape as a single tear traveled down her cheek. Sedro gently pulled at Crosby's shoulder to position her just right to look her in the eyes. "Why the tears, my beautiful girl?" He asked, his voice tender.

Crosby looked up at him with a shaky smile. "I was just wondering if after my journey is complete, will I ever see you again?"

Sedro gazed down at her kindly, brushing a small floret from her hair. "Let's take one step at a time; we can never predict what the future will hold. Remember to stay focused on your needs right now, and let's worry about the rest later."

Crosby whispered; her voice full of emotion. "Sedro, I will miss you a great deal. I have enjoyed singing with you, and I will remember everything that you told me."

As Hansen and Crosby traveled their way out of the meadow, she became thoughtfully curious about the conversation she had with Sedro. "Hansen," she said, "Do you think that Sedro was saying that my smile is not real?"

Hansen glanced down at her; his face thoughtful. "I truly cannot speak for Sedro; I can, however, give you my thoughts on the matter." He replied gently.

"I believe that you believe that your smile is real. You have had to walk through a challenging situation in your young life. Sometimes, when someone has a sudden change in their life, they alter who they are without realizing they are missing a vital piece of who they were. Just remember that as we travel this journey, the experiences you will endure here will become clearer for you and give you understanding and peace. The answers you are seeking will be revealed as we continue through this magical land. I am only here to guide you through this kingdom. The answers will come from the special ones you will meet."

Crosby nodded slowly, taking in his words. After a moment, as Crosby was still pondering on what Hansen had just expressed to her, a thought suddenly occurred to her. "Do you know how many subjects I will meet?" asked Crosby, looking up at him curiously.

Hansen chuckled softly; his eyes warm. "My dear, the journey is adjusted to the length of time it takes for you to confront your truth. Every subject that you will encounter will have vital information for your future."

Crosby thought for a moment, then asked shyly, "Hansen, may I please look into your eyes so that I may check in on my little sister and my dad?"

Hansen smiled and knelt down so that they were at eye level. "Of course, you may, my dear. Would you like to check in on your mother as well?"

Crosby hesitated, then nodded slowly. "I guess it wouldn't hurt to check in on my entire family; thank you, Hansen."

"You're welcome, my darling girl," Hansen replied kindly.

She murmured, her voice tinged with surprise, "Hansen, it looks like they are just going on with their lives like nothing is out of the ordinary."

Hansen gently touched her shoulder. "Crosby, my dear, remember nothing has changed for them; this journey is only for you."

Crosby nodded thoughtfully. "I guess it is going to take a little more time for me to get used to the idea of me being in a magical kingdom while my family continues to do whatever it is that they do throughout the day."

Hansen chuckled softly, and with a gentle nod, they continued on their journey, each step bringing Crosby closer to finding the answers hidden in her heart.

Chapter Fifteen

Miniature Trees

Crosby and Hansen continued along the winding path before them, chatting lightly as they walked. Crosby looked back and noticed the meadow was being left behind, and the land was changing at their feet. That was something that she would not soon get accustomed to seeing and experiencing. The changes in the kingdom were truly far more grand than she could ever express.

"Hansen, are these... miniature trees? She asked, Her eyes wide with delight. She bent down, reaching toward one of the tiny trees. "And may I pull one up?" she asked with a hopeful smile.

Hansen gently shook his head, a soft smile on his face. "Crosby, these are miniature trees. However, you may not pull one up."

Crosby sighed, her eyes still fixed on the little trees. "But Hansen, they are so adorable, and I would like to keep one," she said, her gaze lingering on a particularly charming little tree.

Hansen chuckled, watching her fascination. "Crosby, these trees are deeply rooted in the ground; they are impossible to uproot. They have graced this land for thousands of years. Without these miniature trees, the land will disintegrate; their roots are what keeps our land vibrant and alive."

"Oh well," Crosby murmured, standing back up. "At least I can touch them and admire them while I am here." She reached out, gently brushing her fingers over the soft, tiny branches, but just then, Crosby gasped and rubbed her eyes in disbelief. "Am I seeing things, or are they getting larger as we continue the path?"

Hansen nodded, a knowing glint in his eye. "Yes, they will continue to grow in height as we follow our designated path."

Crosby watched, amazed, as the trees around them stretched up, their trunks thickening and their branches reaching further out. The path began to narrow as the trees grew larger and thicker, the once-clear trail becoming a bit harder to see.

"Hansen, they are getting larger and thicker, and the path is getting harder to see now," she glanced around, gripping her hands together nervously, "I am not sure that we should continue going this way. It is getting a bit harder to feel comfortable on this path." Her breathing was becoming slightly labored. "Do you think that we should turn back before we get lost or even separated," Crosby's breathing was getting more rapid as they continued through the path.

Hansen reached over and gently took her hand in his, giving it a reassuring squeeze. "Crosby," he said softly, looking into her eyes, "The path is altered to what your needs are as we travel. What do you think you need at this moment?"

Crosby hesitated, taking a shaky breath. "I am not sure; will you please just stay close and hold my hand?" She asked quietly, her voice trembling a little.

Hansen smiled gently, his grip firm and warm. "I will. However, I am going to ask you to please take some long, deep breaths with me to calm you down." He inhaled deeply, exhaling slowly, guiding her to do the same. "Is this helping? Are you feeling better?"

Crosby nodded slowly, her breathing evening out as she followed his lead. "Yes, thank you so much," she murmured, giving his hand a grateful squeeze, "I don't know what I would do without you."

Crosby could feel the comfort that Hansen was supplying her. She knew that while she was with Hansen, she could count on him. Hansen nodded, his eyes kind and steady as he looked at her. He could feel her calming down, her grip on his hand loosening slightly as she settled. "Crosby," he said gently, "while you're here in my kingdom, I will always look after you."

Crosby gave him a small, relieved smile, the comfort of his presence steadying her once more. As they continued along the path, surrounded by the towering trees, she felt her heart fill with warmth and gratitude, knowing she could always count on Hansen.

Chapter Sixteen

Erasing Doubt

Crosby continues to walk as closely as possible to Hansen. She felt as though her heart was going to beat out of her chest. The trees were humungous, full, and a very dark green covering the sky so that it was extremely dark and almost damp.

Crosby was struggling to breathe; she was feeling lightheaded, and the fear in her soul was attempting to make her want to quit this journey she was on. Hansen was so great with her. She felt so much better and had the desire to continue even though she still had doubts.

"No need in doubting yourself now, sweetie," Hansen said, reaching out to gently pat her shoulder. "Remember, I am here with you until the end; you can draw strength from me and know that you will never be alone."

Crosby nodded, taking a deep breath. She knew that this journey was imperative for her, even if she was not sure of the full purpose and meaning it had for her future.

She knew that at this point, she needed to embrace her journey and trust the outcome. So, she straightened her back, pulled her shoulders back, and readied herself for what was to come.

As they continued through the forest, Crosby noticed that the trees were changing their colors and thinning out. They were the most vibrant colors she had ever seen in her life. Witnessing these amazing plants and people as she travels through this kingdom is making her wish that she could stay here forever.

"Hansen, these trees are gorgeous!" she exclaimed, running her hand over a branch. "I love the colors, and they make me feel safe somehow." She looked up at him, a smile lighting her face.

Hansen knew that Crosby was allowing herself to find comfort in the atmosphere around her. This was good because it is very important in her journey for her to trust. Since the change of events in her family's home life, Crosby has had a difficult time trusting anything lately.

Hansen smiled gently, watching her. "Yes, it's good to see you finding comfort in your surroundings," he replied, his tone warm. He placed a hand on her shoulder. "It's very important for your journey that you trust and allow yourself to feel at ease here."

As Crosby's doubt dissipated and her confidence grew, she felt light and airy as she continued down the path. She did not realize how the change in her atmosphere was contributing to her lack of doubt. She wondered if she would continue to feel like this even after she left this kingdom.

Hansen watched her closely, wondering if she would express her feelings about what she was thinking. Just as he was going to engage in conversation, Crosby took a deep breath and confronted her fears to Hansen.

"Hansen, When I go home, will I be able to feel the same peace I feel here?"

"When we reach the end, you will feel more than just peace as you return home. However, I need you to focus on the here and now. You will be able to process everything you need for your life if you stay focused."

Chapter Seventeen

Majestic Lake

As the trees began to thin out, a beautiful lake of purpled waters began to appear; this was giving her a form of relief. The beauty of its majesty transformed before their eyes as the sun rays glistened across the lake; its deep, purpled water transcended into an iridescent fuchsia with golden speckles.

Crosby gasped, her hand over her mouth. "Hansen, look at that!" she whispered, awe filling her voice.

Hansen nodded, his gaze soft. "Isn't it beautiful?" he asked, turning to her with a gentle smile.

They reach a fork in the path that branched out in four directions, each indistinguishable from the next. Crosby came to an abrupt halt at the site of the forked paths. "Hansen, which path do we take now," she said, her voice shaking a little. "They all look the same!" She looked up at him, searching his face for guidance.

"Crosby, each path has its own designated journey neither path is incorrect." Hansen replied, giving her hand a reassuring squeeze.

"How are we supposed to choose then?" She asked, glancing between the paths anxiously. She fidgeted, rubbing her hands together.

"The choice is yours alone; I cannot help you choose," Hansen replied.

"How do I choose?" Crosby looked up once again for the guidance.

"Close your eyes, listen to your heart; it will lead us in the right direction," Hansen suggested, smiling kindly.

Crosby impatiently walked back and forth, scratching at her head, grunting, and gasping. She knew that if her mother were with her at this moment, she would scold her for making non-lady-like noises. She wondered if her mother would have known that this was a crucial decision she had to make on her own. For some reason unknown to her, she wished her mother was with her right now to make this decision.

"Hansen, I am scared; what if I make the wrong decision?" Said Crosby. "What if I choose, and it happens to be an entirely different path that I am meant to follow?"

Hansen gently cupped her shoulder, bending down slightly to meet her eyes. "My dear Crosby, when you listen to your heart, you will hear its true revelation; remember, there isn't a wrong decision." He said softly.

Crosby stood there still in silence, studying all the paths carefully for what felt like hours, which truly were only about ten minutes. However, she was not in the mindset to contemplate the actual concept of time, especially since she was in a different world altogether; she was engrossed in only making the correct decision no matter how much Hansen told her she couldn't be wrong, no matter which she chose.

She was engrossed in only making the correct decision no matter how much Hansen told her she couldn't be wrong, no matter which she chose.

The reason she was having a difficult time making this decision is because, in her world, she was always taught that there is a wrong or right in the decisions that you make daily. Her mother always tells her before she leaves the house to make good choices. This was a bit difficult for her to take in and understand. She told herself that she was in a magical kingdom, and everything was upside down. "Crosby," Hansen startled her out of her deep thoughts. "The reason there is not a right or wrong here has nothing to do with the differences in our worlds. You should always try to make good choices. This decision is tailored to your needs, this is why there is no right or wrong this time. It only means that whichever path you take will determine the subjects you will encounter."

"Okay' that makes more sense to me now; by the way, it is still surprising to me that you can read my thoughts. I am thankful; I'm just not sure that I will ever get used to that. I will forever be grateful for having this experience. I know it's not over, but it is amazing and special."

Chapter Eighteen

Meeting Tailey

She extended her arms as if to welcome the wisdom she was seeking; her long, dark, beautiful eyelashes rested on her olive skin, gently hugging the tip of her cheekbones. As her eyes slowly opened, a shy smile encompassed her face; she knew exactly which path to take without any hesitation. Although this confused Crosby, she still obeyed the orders she had been given.

With a poised confidence in her stance, which has been asleep for a while, Crosby pointed towards the third path and said, "Hansen, we need to follow this one."

Hansen's eyes sparkled as he returned her smile. "That sounds perfect," he said, gently guiding her toward the chosen path.

Hansen was pleased to know that Crosby would be encountering some interesting characters in his kingdom. As they followed through on the path, Crosby stepped onto the water; she noticed that the golden speckles were turning into golden lily pads underneath her feet.

Excitement overtaking her emotions, Crosby screeched, "Hansen, look over there in the middle of the lake!"

Hansen was calm and asked, "Crosby, what do you see, my dear."

"That almost looks like a frog, but I have never seen a frog quite like that one. Will I get to speak with that amazingly beautiful frog?" Crosby replied, still amazed.

Hansen's smile widened, and he nodded. "Crosby, as I said before, we will only encounter that which is conducive to your healing process."

Crosby was mesmerized by the golden lilies underneath her feet; she was so enthralled by them, giggling and skipping, enjoying her youth that she hardly noticed how close to the center of the lake they were.

Just then, a clear voice echoed across the lake. "Please stop where you stand; do not take another step."

Crosby was so startled at the sound of someone's voice that Hansen was forced to reach out and hold her from falling into the lake. She looked up to see a large pink frog dotted with black spots that shimmered in the sun.

"Oh my, I am so sorry to intrude and interrupt you, ma'am; I didn't mean to be so rude." The frog, whose voice was surprisingly warm, gave her a friendly nod.

"Hello, Crosby, my name is Tailey," she croaked softly, "And you have not intruded on me in any way. I could tell that you were genuinely enjoying my home; I wanted to ensure that you and I got a chance to chat before you ran past me in a haze. I only stopped you because to continue your fabulous journey, you will need to follow my instructions."

Crosby took a cautious step forward, her eyes wide with curiosity. "Yes, of course, Tailey," she replied, hands nervously twisting in front of her. "What do we need to talk about?"

Tailey was a three-foot-tall pink frog with black dots all over her body that glistened when the sun shone on them at just the right angle; her eyes were a brilliant purple with a magical fuchsia color circling the pupil of her eyes. She sits on a large golden lily pad with an enormous rainbow-feathered trellis, which protects her from the elements and shoots tiny pieces of food into the lake for all the dancing tadpoles.

Tailey requests the presence of Crosby's attention so that they can discuss the next steps in her journey. Tailey informs Crosby that she is to take only two steps at a time and then stop so that the lily pads can reveal the direction of the conversation they are to have.

However, her curiosity does not fail her. She wonders as she stands still on the golden pad how the lily pads will change colors. She wonders if it will be a gradual change or if it will turn immediately after stepping on them. "You will not get the answer to your thoughts if you just stand there and wonder,

my dear," said Hansen. She takes a deep, cleansing breath to
continue on her journey.

Chapter Nineteen

Changing Colors

Although this confused Crosby, she still obeyed the orders she had been given. Crosby took two steps; the lily pad underneath her was now bright red with golden streaks woven into its veins.

She was startled when she saw that the most elegant flowers began to appear all around her. The flowers were a single large crimson-red silk leaf with a silver stem, and the pistil was a radiant mixture of red and orange fur-like appearance.

Each flower was only different in size. However, each one held a different scent, which gave the atmosphere a mysterious aroma.

Crosby looked up at Tailey with confusion in her eyes as she muttered a question to Tailey. "Tailey, why did the lily pad turn red when I stepped on it?"

Tailey gazed at her kindly, her voice full of understanding. "Crosby, something in your life has made you feel extreme animosity toward a loved one. Would you like to share with me where the problem lies?" She tilted her head, watching her carefully.

Crosby shook her head quickly, laughing nervously. "Oh, Tailey, I do not have any resentment towards anyone; my life is fine." She said, her fingers twisting at her sleeve.

"Crosby, I believe now is a suitable time for me to tell you that I possess the gift of reading minds. I chose not to reveal this in hopes that you would be truthful with me." Tailey's eyes softened.

Taking a deep breath, Crosby glanced down, her hands trembling slightly. "Tailey, I am afraid that if I speak my mind, I will be judged and criticized as a single tear rolled down her cheek."

"Crosby, this is a safe place for you," she assured her, her voice like a warm embrace, "We are all here to help you follow and complete your journey without any judgment. However, we cannot assist you if you do not entrust your innermost secrets with us." She gave Crosby an encouraging nod, her gaze gentle. "I realize that sharing your feelings has been something of a struggle for you lately, but you must find the courage to finally release your emotions without holding back, no matter how devasting you may think they are."

Crosby began to search her heart; even though it was not too difficult to pinpoint the depths of her rage, she took a moment to reflect on and embrace the courage she was seeking.

Crosby took a deep, cleansing breath before she decided to share her story with Tailey and Hansen. She began softly, the words tumbling out. "My parents started arguing a lot before I turned 7 years old. They never knew that most times I could hear them and was protecting my sister from hearing their arguments. The fighting only got worse, and then they decided to get a divorce," Crosby continued, "My dad moved out of the house, and mom allowed Jason to move into our home."

Tailey nodded, listening intently, her gaze never wavering.

Crosby's eyes filled with tears as she remembered. "His presence in our life and moving in with us was so fast for us that we didn't understand how our mom could do this to our dad. My sister and I were informed that we were to consider and address Jason as our new father. I chose to express my feelings to my mother, informing her that I only have one dad, and this made her incredibly angry. I knew that she was disappointed in me, and she began to be displeased with my actions toward them; it didn't matter much to me anyway because I didn't like her actions much either." She looked up at Hansen, who gave her a gentle, supportive smile.

"Every time my dad would call, my mom was very cruel to him, which I believe is due to my attitude towards her boyfriend." She paused, letting the words sink in.

Crosby's mind took her to that day when her mom was on the phone with her dad before she went to school. Her mother's sudden gush of fury and harsh criticism towards her dad awakened and increased the agony in her heart.

Crosby began to gasp for air and saw white spots before her eyes. A fountain of tears streamed down her flushed pink cheeks, drenching the neckline of her pink-laced blouse. Her second horrifying memory was of the day that her dad left her house. She could see how broken he was feeling just by the way his shoulders were slumped and he was hanging his head.

"I told my mother that I hated her, and I will never be able to forgive her." Hansen began to soothe her and calm her spirit.

When she was fully calmed, Tailey addressed her with warmth and love in her voice; it had been a while since Crosby had heard a tender, motherly voice directed at her.

Chapter Twenty

Release of Feelings

Tailey moved closer, her voice tender and full of warmth. "My dear Crosby, your pain has been imprisoned far too long. When your mother left your father for another man, you chose to lock it into your heart and expected to forget about the pain." She paused, then continued again, "The choice of your words towards your mother was harsh, and you are having a difficult time dealing with that. There is not a person on the planet that can endure such pain without losing a part of themself. Now that you have released that anger, would you like to learn how to put it behind you?"

Crosby nodded, a small, hopeful smile breaking through her tears. "Yes, I would, Tailey. I love my mother very much, but I would appreciate it if I were able to like her as well. I also wonder if she will ever have it in her heart to forgive me," she whispered, her hand clenching tightly as she looked up at Tailey.

Tailey's gaze softened, and she nodded approvingly. "Crosby, you must first forgive yourself in order to receive the forgiveness of your mother only then will you have an open heart and mind."

"When I do forgive myself, how long will it take for me to feel it working in my heart?" Crosby asked.

"Crosby, when the heart transcends all understanding it is felt lighter, and one is at peace with themselves," Tailey instructed.

"Are you ready to move further? Are you ready to let it go?" Tailey asked.

"Yes, ma'am, I am," Crosby replied.

"Okay, please take two more steps towards me, Crosby," Tailey instructed her again.

When Crosby took her two steps forward closer to Tailey, she realized that the flowers around her began to disappear, and the lily pad she was now standing on was an orange and red paisley design.

Tailey watched her with a gentle smile, her posture relaxed and welcoming. "Remember, Crosby," she said softly. "Forgiveness begins with yourself."

The water was rippling in a circular motion, and tiny rainbow-colored tadpoles were dancing in the water as if the waters were magically producing music. It was as if the silent music was calming her spirit.

Tailey's posture was pivoted into a gentler stance, which gave Crosby the sign of comfort she was searching for. She could feel the warmth and acceptance of Tailey's heart. It had been a long time since she had felt this comfort; she felt an overwhelming peace and yet still felt a minor amount of grief. She realized that the grief could only be stemming from the outburst she had endured during her argument with her mother.

Crosby felt as though maybe there was still some hope of mending her relationship with her mother; she just needed help to figure out the best way to handle this situation.

She was desperate to learn and soak in everything that Hansen and Tailey would do to help her get to that point. She feels the need to be a normal person, which really, she doesn't truly know the real definition of what normal would be.

Crosby closed her eyes, her heart feeling just a little lighter. She looked up, smiling through her tears, as a sense of peace began to settle over her.

Chapter Twenty-One

Struggling With Acceptance

Crosby watched the tadpoles dance in silence for a while, the gentle rhythm of their movement was helping to calm her nerves. She observed them closely, noticing each time they leaped from the water, a slight shift in their rainbow hues. The change was not significant; however, it was noticeable if one was paying attention to them.

She wondered if somehow the tadpoles had any significance to her healing. Tailey and Hansen quietly watched as Crosby studied the tadpoles; they knew this was a therapeutic and vital moment for Crosby to take possession of her feelings. The next steps in her journey would involve learning acceptance for her struggles, with Tailey's guidance helping her see that her feelings were valid in the context of her experience. She will teach her that although her words towards her mother were harsh, it was the only way she knew to express herself in that moment.

As Tailey watched Crosby, she decided to address her about moving forward on her journey.

"Crosby," Tailey said softly, "Are you ready to move forward?"

Crosby took a shaky breath and looked at her, hesitating. "Tailey, is it possible for me to take a little more time before we move forward? I feel as though I need to settle my nerves just a little more. Remembering my argument with my mom has left me unstable and shaky."

"Of course, Crosby, you take as much time as you need," Tailey responded with a gentle smile, "Let us know when you are ready to move forward. This is your journey, and we want you to be as comfortable and confident as you can be," Tailey continued, "This is only molding you and preparing you for when you return home."

Crosby had taken another thirty minutes to regroup her thoughts. When she felt stronger and more prepared to move forward, she looked up at Tailey and told her she was ready.

But then she hesitated, taking a deep breath before addressing Hansen, "Hansen, may I look into your eyes?" She asked hesitantly, "I want to see how my mom is doing before I move on, please."

Hansen's expression softened, and he gave a small nod. "Of course, you may, my dear."

Crosby's gaze turned intense as she peered into Hansen's eyes, searching. "Hansen, she looks really sad right now, could she be thinking about our relationship?"

Hansen's expression grew thoughtful. "I don't know what is on her mind, sweetheart; I am only able to read minds in my kingdom."

A tinge of disappointment crossed Crosby's face. "Okay, maybe we should just go forward; maybe it will change as we continue on the path."

"Crosby," Tailey pointed out, "Have you noticed that the lily pad that you are now standing on has changed colors?"

Crosby looked down in surprise, "Yes, Tailey, but I was wondering why there is still red woven in this one. You said that the red was due to my anger. Does this mean that my anger is still not completely gone?"

"You're right, Crosby," Tailey said with a knowing look. "The colors of the lily pad reflect your inner state. You see, our minds reflect the ripples in the water; as we become resentful, it becomes muddy and impossible to see, but when we allow the water to settle, our minds become clearer, our choices become apparent and easier to make."

Crosby sighed, her face clouded with worry, "How can I get rid of all my anger towards my mom?"

Tailey smiled gently, her tone understanding, "When you remember that the choice is not yours to make. Your mom made some adult choices; you will never understand the choices a grownup makes; you are a child, and it is not your job to understand. The only thing that you must do is remember that everyone makes mistakes even if we are confident in our choices. Your mom's choices may not be correct in your eyes, but for her, choosing happiness with Jason was important to her. It had been a long time since she was happy with your father; she felt the need to make a choice to try and bring a semblance of happiness back into your home. Maybe she felt that divorcing your dad and finding happiness with Jason would help her mend the loss of the love she had felt for your dad once upon a time. Maybe she didn't realize how truly difficult it was going to be for her to let go. I know that you feel that she made this choice without thinking of her children, but since you nor I can read her mind, we truly don't know whether or not she considered your feelings."

As Crosby contemplated the words that Tailey expressed, she allowed her mind to wander. It is true that she will never understand the reason that her mother has for leaving her father and not knowing if she thought what it would do to her children, so why does she still feel compelled to hold on to the anger?

Chapter Twenty-Two

Letting Go

"Tailey, do you know how long it will take for me to understand my anger towards my mother?" She asked softly, almost pleading.

"You are well on your way to cutting the anger from your heart. There is still more work to be done before your goal is reached." Replied Tailey. "Crosby, our feelings are a vital part of our mental growth no matter the emotion. Understanding and expressing our feelings help us to stay healthy mentally. Sometimes, we are made to believe that anger is a horrible expression and should be kept hidden. Expressing your anger is okay as long as you don't allow it to engulf your life."

Tailey's expression was warm. "I can only promise that as you continue your journey, you will be provided with methods that will help you accept your feelings. Even if you leave here without fully understanding and letting go of your anger, we will help you embrace a healthier way to express yourself and have a better relationship with your mother."

Crosby took a moment to reflect on what Tailey had just told her; she was looking out over the horizon, just gazing at nothing and everything. "Tailey, when I go home, I want to be able to feel comfortable to talk to all the grown-ups that are in my life without feeling guilty. I was thinking about how I like Jason; I want to be able to have a real relationship with him since he is going to be with my mom. I know that he wants to have a relationship with us as well; my anger has not allowed me to give him a chance. I have also made sure to feed my sister so much negative about Jason that she also is not receptive to his kindness. I guess I was just feeling like we shouldn't be told that we have to love or like someone just because they are now a part of my life. I like being happy, and I want to wear a real smile again. Do you think that's possible, even after all the hurt in our family?"

Tailey's eyes glistened with understanding, "Crosby, the changes your family must endure will only be successful if everyone in the family is willing to participate with an open and willing heart. We will work with you to be able to get everything in motion; true healing begins with one person's willingness to accept their own faults in the equation. You are well on your way in achieving this goal in your life and your family's lives."

As Crosby stepped forward onto the next lily pad, she noticed the red fading and hints of yellow starting to appear. The lily pad was now orange and yellow. With wide eyes, she looked up at Tailey in amazement. "Tailey, look the red is gone from the lily pad! Is this because I am changing and willing to let go of my anger?"

"Yes, Crosby," Tailey said with a warm smile. "But notice that the orange has darkened; this means that although the red is completely gone, you still have a hint of anger. Please understand that it will take more time; you are well on your way to cutting the anger from your heart. Crosby, aside from the way that your mom treats your dad, is there anything else that makes you feel uncomfortable? I can only help you if you continue to open your heart to me." Crosby paused thoughtfully. "Tailey, I am not sure if this is something that is making me angry. I do know that it makes me stay awake at night. When my mom demanded that we call Jason dad, I let her know that I would only ever have one dad. I feel as though she does not like me for not listening to her. She and I were very close at one time, and now she barely talks to me."

Chapter Twenty-Three

The Healing Continues

Hansen stepped in, his tone filled with empathy. "In time, Crosby, the adults in your family will hopefully learn to treat each other with respect. As a child, you should not have to worry about such huge emotions in your life; your sole job should be to enjoy school, your friends, and your family. This is the time in your life when you should be learning about who you really want to become. The way you have spoken to me about your father, I feel as though he would never want you to struggle with whether or not you should love Jason. Your father's only wish is that you be happy and that Jason will always treat you well."

Crosby's lips trembled as she replied, "I am sure that you are right about this, Hansen; it is just hard for me; I want to learn to love Jason, but I feel like if I do, I will be betraying my father, it is difficult to believe that my dad will not feel betrayed."

Hansen watched Crosby closely, sensing her distress. "Crosby, please remember that it is not your job to make sure that your father is happy."

"And as for your mom," Tailey added softly, "Your mom has never stopped liking or loving you. When you told her that you hate her, it penetrated to the core of her heart. The hurt your mother's feelings is very deep; it is also consumed with guilt for what she has put you and your sister through. Her pain and guilt have altered her way of addressing you, which comes across as dislike. Your mother will also need to search her heart to release this, to allow herself to respect herself enough to accept her faults in the transition of your family. She will also need to mend her relationship with your father for you and your sister's sake. When she takes these steps to better her family, things will become easier for your family. Your role in this is simply to forgive her and allow your hearts to mend. You are not the peacemaker of your family."

"Tailey, if I am not the peacemaker, why am I here? Crosby asked, her voice tinged with confusion. "How do I help my family heal?"

Tailey's face softened as she leaned in closer. "As you progress in this journey, things will become clearer for you. It is important for you to continue to focus on your needs first, and everything else will fall into place."

"Since we already know why I lost my smile, does this mean that I am going back to my desk now?" Crosby asked with a hint of anticipation.

"Not yet, Crosby," Tailey answered kindly. "Just because something is brought to the surface does not mean that there is a resolution."

"How will we know that everything is resolved?"

"When you reach the High Commander, you will have received all the information and some knowledge that you will need to restore your family. So, I want you to keep in mind what I told you, focus on your needs first."

Crosby took a deep breath, letting the words settle in her heart. She felt a glimmer of hope as she looked out over the water, her eyes reflecting the soft glow of the orange and yellow lily pad beneath her feet.

Chapter Twenty-Four

Reflecting

After Hansen and Crosby ended their conversation with Tailey, they said their goodbyes and continued their journey. Hansen noticed that Crosby was rather quiet as they moved further away from the lake.

"I will miss that beautiful lake," Crosby murmured a wistful note in her voice. "I have never seen such a lake as that one. Will I see anything like that again? Do I have to leave this place? I am very happy here; there are so many beautiful areas, and I am making wonderful, unique friends. If I cannot stay here, will I still be able to have contact with them and you?"

Hansen looked like he was a million miles away for a moment; Crosby had a confused look on her face as she watched him mull over a few things. Crosby was full of questions, and although he had the answers, he feared that Crosby was not fully ready for the answers. He placed his right-wing over his beak to ensure that he handled these questions with care and comfort.

"Crosby," he began gently, "We still have quite a bit of time together. Let's just focus on this moment; the future has the potential to change without any notice.

Crosby was so deep in thought that she had not noticed that her surroundings were quickly transforming and revealing a new type of countryside. Crosby had come across many different beautiful landscapes; this area was the most unique type of woodland she had ever seen. Although she had seen the smallest of trees with deep-rooted roots and trees so large and full of very little space in between them, these woodlands were so special and extremely welcoming.

The trees had a thick, clear trunk in which you could see the teal roots traveling into the ground. The roots were constantly stimulating the trunk with a steady flow running through in a backward motion. The trees did not have leaves like the last ones had. Instead, they were small balls with prickly points all around and of every color you could imagine.

The trees were no more than a foot tall. Crosby was so excited with the fact that she was able to watch as tiny birds landed on the balls. As she watched, she noticed that each bird would deposit something bright yellow into the balls.

A spark lit up in Crosby's eyes. "Hansen, this is beautiful; please explain to me what the birds are doing?"

Hansen smiled, pleased by her excitement. "Crosby, these birds are so small, and their sole purpose is to pollinate our dulse trees."

"Pollinate trees?" Crosby asked, eyebrows raised in surprise. "I thought only flowers needed pollination." "

"These are rare trees, my dear; these trees are where our entire kingdom receives its nourishment," Hansen explained, a note of pride in his voice.

A thoughtful look crossed Crosby's face. "Hansen, I just realized that the entire time I have been here, I haven't been thirsty or hungry. Does this mean that while I am here, I, too, receive nourishment through these trees?"

Hansen nodded knowingly. "Crosby, if you recall, when you came through that door in your classroom, I informed you that you were now in a magical kingdom. In this place, we all receive nourishment in the same manner; there is no reason for you to worry about things you generally worry about in your world." Hansen continued, "Our universes are completely different; while in your world, you live by schedules for everything concerning your health; here, it is all maintained by our dulce trees and their keepers."

Crosby's eyes widened in amazement. "Wow, that's really cool; if my world was like that, I would have a lot more time to do whatever I wanted."

Hansen's gaze softened. "You see, sweetie, in your world, when one is given a privilege, it is generally not appreciated. One is always wanting more than they are gifted and instead looks for more; therefore, it is rarely deserved."

Chapter Twenty-Five

Meeting Rehn

Crosby thought about what Hansen had just said. Her mind wandered back to a moment when she asked her parents for something specific, and when she received it, she was still searching for more.

"Hansen," she began softly, her voice tinged with shame, "I am so ashamed because I have done that many times in my life. I don't want to be that person!"

Hansen's warm gaze reassured her, but before he could respond, Crosby heard a buzzing around her that was extremely loud. She stopped to see if she could find the source of that buzzing. She then noticed a bird a bit larger than the ones that were pollinating the trees. He was just perched up on one of the balls and looking straight at Crosby.

Crosby began to feel a little self-conscious. She felt as if she was strategically being watched. She turned toward Hansen, intending to ask about the bird and her uneasy feelings, when a booming voice shattered the stillness. She jumped and nearly fell over; however, Hansen caught her before she could fall.

To her surprise, the voice belonged to the tiny bird sitting on one of the balls. When she paid more attention to the voice, she realized he was addressing her.

"Oh, hi," she managed, her voice shaky but polite.

At that moment, Hansen realized that there was an exchange happening and made sure to make the introductions.

"Crosby, this is Rehn, and Rehn, this is Crosby."

"I know who she is," Rehn replied, his voice commanding but not unkind.

Hansen raised a feathered brow, "I'm being polite. Will that do for you, sir?"

Rehn gave a slight tilt of his head as if amused.

Crosby blinked at the exchange, then looked back at Rehn with astonishment.

"Rehn, your voice is... um kind of intimidating," she admitted, her eyes were as big as saucers.

"Oh! I'm sorry, dear," Rehn said, his tone rough but carrying an unmistakable tenderness. "I do not have volume control; this is just who I am."

Crosby smiled, relaxing a little, "It's okay, I think that I can get used to it... it just caught me off guard."

Rehn was a blackbird with teal-tipped feathers; his feet were purple with teal claws. His eyes were golden with teal speckles around the pupils; his beak was gold with a single half-teal and half-purple triangle at the tip. He was the size of a hummingbird. His voice was loud, strong, and rough; however, you could hear the tenderness in it as he spoke.

Crosby was having a really hard time. She knew that it was rude to stare, but Rehn was such a beautiful bird that she couldn't stop staring. Finally, she said, "You're so beautiful and rare. I'm sorry, but I can't stop staring."

Rehn tilted his head in wonderment and said, "It's okay, my dear; I do realize that we are all a rare breed for you. I'm sure that you have never encountered anything like any of us in your world."

"You are so correct," Crosby admitted with a little laugh. "I have never seen anything like all of you nor the beautiful landscapes I have seen during this journey. I feel very privileged to be able to experience this kingdom."

Rehn's golden eyes glimmered, "Crosby, I am very pleased that you have enjoyed our kingdom. At this moment, we need to talk about what brought you here."

Crosby nodded, her expression turning serious, "Yes, all of you have been very kind and understanding. I do have a question or more of a wonderment if you, please. Something that Sedro told me has been weighing on my heart."

Rehn leaned forward slightly, his gaze encouraging, "Oh, what is it that is a concern for you, my dear?"

"Well," Crosby began, hesitating for a moment, "Sedro told me that I wouldn't understand my drawing on the board until I am ready. And... I think I am ready now. I believe I understand it."

Rehn's feathers ruffled slightly, a sign of interest, "Do you feel as though you are ready to talk about that portion of your drawing, dear?"

Crosby took a deep breath, "I am not only ready, but I think that I understand what it means."

"Okay, well then, let's talk about that portion of the drawing. What do you believe is your interpretation of the thorns?"

With deep breaths taken in, Crosby started, "You see, I was angry at my mother when I was drawing it. I had overheard her yelling at my dad for wanting to pick us up after school for my birthday. When she acts like that towards my dad, it hurts me, and I think that I hate her." Her voice cracked, and she quickly added, "So, do you believe that this is a symbol of hatred?"

Rehn's gaze softened. "What do you feel when she does that, Crosby?"

"She makes me feel as though I can't breathe," Crosby confessed, her voice trembling. "I feel like I don't want her around us anymore. I think that since the thorns demonstrate pain, I believe that I was just thinking that maybe I want her to feel the pain that I am feeling. I don't like that I feel like that. Does that make me a horrible person?"

Rehn's voice was calm but firm, "Crosby, you are a young girl with many unexpected feelings. Most grown-ups going through a divorce have worse feelings about each other than what you are feeling now. This does not make you a horrible person; it's the only way you know to express yourself."

As Crosby watched the birds fly all around the beautiful trees, she wondered what it would take for her to feel the peace she was feeling now when she returned to her world.

Rehn's voice broke through her reverie, "You know, Crosby, when you forgive yourself for the feelings you had towards your mother, that is when you will be able to forgive her. Your pain is very real and shameless; once you and your mother can reunite and talk about your feelings, you will have the peace you are searching for. Also, you must know that when you forgive someone for their actions or words, forgiveness isn't about them. The forgiveness is for your healing. Once you heal it will give you a better understanding of their feelings."

Crosby's head snapped up, startled, "Okay, wait, I haven't said a word! Does this mean that you can hear my thoughts as well?"

Rehn chuckled, the sound softer than before, "I cannot hear your thoughts; however, Hansen and I can mentally communicate. "Hansen let me know what you are thinking. I just felt it was important for you to hear my thoughts on this instead of Hansen's."

Crosby blinked at Hansen, who offered her a reassuring nod.

"Crosby, when you return to your world," Rehn continued, "It will be very important for you to embrace and practice everything that you have learned here on your journey. I do realize that you have enjoyed and been awed by the different things you have experienced. Know that when you are home, you will be able to remember your journey. Although you will remember everything, it will only be as if it happened in a dream. Please remember that in your world, a dream is difficult to explain; this is true when it comes to your journey."

Crosby frowned slightly, "Will I remember everything or only portions of my journey?"

"You remember only what you need at the exact time that you will need it," Rehn said gently, "Okay, I feel as though I'm not going to get any further with this now. I will just wait and enjoy the rest of my time."

Rehn continued, "Crosby, the more you attempt to jam everything that has happened, the easier it will be deleted from your memory. Always remember to breathe and take one step at a time."

Crosby sighed but nodded, "Okay, Rehn, I will do as you say. I can't promise that I will always remember that since I am a child."

Rehn's golden eyes sparkled with amusement, "I am well aware of this, my child; this is why I am letting you know that you will have spurts of memories for as long as you need them and when you need them the most."

Chapter Twenty-Six

Enjoying Rehn and His Friends

After having such a heavy conversation, Rehn tilted his head and asked Crosby with a mischievous glint in his golden eyes, "Would you like to enjoy my land to the fullest?"

Crosby's brows furrowed in confusion as she blinked up at him. "Rehn, what do you mean by that? Your land is already incredible. How could I enjoy it even more?"

Rehn continued with a jolly smile on his face, "Crosby, my land has a special feature that you will not believe. You can enjoy it with more than just your eyes. There is a way for you to almost feel as though you are at an amusement park."

"Okay, now I need you to start talking and tell me what you mean by that!" Crosby replied; she was full of curiosity.

Hansen and Rehn began to laugh so hard that Rehn's voice was shaking the ground. Crosby's eyes grew extremely large at the sensation of the shaking ground.

"Rehn! Are you trying to shake me up on purpose?" she exclaimed, placing her hands on her hips. Rehn fluttered his wings dramatically. "Oh no, dear child, just an uncontrollable reaction. My voice does tend to rattle things a bit when I'm thoroughly amused!" Hansen, now shaking with silent laughter, muttered, "You might want to get used to that."

As soon as they settled down, Rehn began the process. "Now, let's begin." He raised his head and issued a series of melodic calls, summoning his feathered friends to prepare the land for Crosby to enjoy.

Immediately, they began to fly inches apart from each other. As Crosby watched, she noticed that not only were they flying close together, but something was also forming underneath them. The roots in the trees began to form colorful swings, and Crosby thought to herself with a surprised facial expression, is that a waterslide that is forming? Crosby is so excited that she begins to jump up and down and make a screeching sound, which makes Hansen flutter his wings for the first time since she got there. It startled Crosby; then she realized that her screeching had caught him off guard.

For the first time, Crosby noticed that the inside of Hansen's wings was shining with silver-like glitter all over. Crosby looked up at Hansen and said, "You're even more stunning than I thought."

Hansen smiled warmly, folding his wings back, "Thank you, Crosby." Crosby told Hansen that she thought that was the most incredible place she has ever seen.

"I think you might want to turn your attention back to Rehn and his friends." Hansen directed her attention to more beautiful scenery.

She turned her attention to the birds to see what else they were developing. As Crosby takes a closer look, she realizes that there is something different about this waterslide. On the waterslide she notices that it is not water that is coming down from the slide. The roots are producing a glittery type of liquid. Is that really Jell-O with glitter that she is seeing? She begins to take a step towards the slide and is held back by Hansen.

"Crosby," he said gently but firmly, "You must let the process continue without any disturbance. The birds that are working to make this wonderland happen cannot be touched. The moment these birds are touched by anything foreign, they will lose their breath and cease to exist due to the contamination."

The expression on Crosby's face was more than comical. Her eyes widened in horror. Hansen couldn't help but giggle at her as she continued to watch the birds work on the slide and other amenities.

"Oh no! I didn't mean to disturb them!" Her voice was tinged with guilt, but Hansen shook his head with a kind smile.

"You haven't done anything wrong, Crosby," Hansen replied with a warm smile.

Crosby raised one more concern, "Hansen, how much longer do we have to wait until we can enjoy this place?"

"Oh, Crosby, there is no we in this scenario; you will take advantage of this on your own," Hansen replied.

"Well, that's no fun for you, but I will not pass on this opportunity. I plan on enjoying myself until I am utterly exhausted!" Just as Hansen was about to respond to Crosby's statement, Rehn fluttered onto Hansen's shoulder, "Hansen, you are such a fuddy-duddy. This dear child will have to entertain herself all because you can't be bothered to enjoy yourself for once."

Hansen shot Rehn an unimpressed glance, "Rehn, you know that I am too large to get on any of the wonderful contraptions your legion of fowl has constructed."

"Oh, I know..." Rehn replied with a dramatic sigh. "I just enjoy seeing you squirm. You make it so easy, my friend."

Hansen simply gave Rehn a displeased look and went about discussing the area with Crosby.

"Just one thing to note," Hansen added, his tone light. "As you go about enjoying this park, you will be covered in a slime and glitter substance. Also, know that the moment you are finished enjoying yourself and removing yourself, you will no longer have any evidence of the glitter and slime substance on your body."

Crosby gasped dramatically. "Wait... you're telling me I can get all messy and not have to clean up afterward? This just became the *coolest* thing I've ever done!"

"Oh, I thought it was the small trees, the lake, or even the dancing frogs," Hansen laughed and replied.

"Oh, everything has been amazing; it's just that getting all dirty and not having to clean up afterward is more than amazing!" Crosby added her point.

Hansen chuckled, shaking his head, "You have just reminded me of how young you truly are, my dear."

"Is that bad?" Crosby asked, tilting her head curiously.

"Not good or bad, just a reminder, my dear," Hansen said with a soft smile.

Crosby lifted her head up and smiled at Hansen before she ran off to play in this beautiful and exciting area.

Crosby played for a while and was exhausted. Reluctantly, she left the park area to meet up with Rehn and Hansen.

As she walked towards them, they noticed that she had some tears rolling down her cheeks. Hansen immediately knew why the stream of tears was falling. Rehn, however, worried that maybe she had gotten hurt while playing in the wonderland.

"Crosby, are you hurt?" Rehn asked, his booming voice unusually tender.

Crosby shook her head, wiping her tears with the back of her hand. "No, I'm not hurt," she said softly. "I'm just... I'm going to miss this place so much."

Rehn's feathers seemed to shimmer even brighter as he leaned forward, his tone gentle. "Oh, my dear, we will miss you too. It has been an honor to meet you."

Crosby carefully cupped Rehn in her hands, smiling through her tears. "You're the best bird I've ever met."

"And you, Crosby, are one of the most remarkable children I've ever encountered," Rehn replied with heartfelt sincerity.

Hansen simply watched, his expression serene, as the moment passed between them, knowing this memory would stay with Crosby long after her journey ended.

Chapter Twenty-Seven

Journey To the Higher Commander

Hansen and Crosby continued their journey through the land one more time. This time, leaving Rehn and the wonderland behind. As they walked Crosby took the opportunity to excitedly share her experience in the wonderland with Hansen.

Crosby was so engrossed with her story that she did not notice that the land was changing under her feet. Hansen continued to listen intently to her story, knowing that it was extremely important to give Crosby his undivided attention. As she was telling her story, she realized that something was changing. She immediately stopped when she realized that the ground beneath her was different. Crosby rambled, but she suddenly halted mid-sentence. Her wide eyes darted to the ground, and she gasped, her voice trembling with surprise.

Crosby gasped as she realized that the ground was soft and furry. "Hansen, do you see this? The ground—it's... soft? And furry?!"

Hansen's lips curved into a knowing smirk, but he said nothing, watching her reaction.

The green and silver-bladed grass also felt velvety and was breathtakingly beautiful.

Her eyes widened even further when she noticed the flowers nearby. "Hansen!" she exclaimed, pointing excitedly. "Those flowers... they almost look like bats! They're extraordinary!"

Hansen folded his arms and tilted his head, clearly enjoying her enthusiasm. "Oh? Extraordinary, you say? Why don't you tell me exactly what you see, my dear?"

The head has a unique shape; the top is pointed, and at the top of the peak, it is split, flaring out left and right. As you follow the peak down it splits open and expands one foot wide and resembles a floppy sun hat. In the center of the split it has a gold diamond that connects the two. It is a furry violet color with snow-white speckles and severed edges.

The brown face has four points and is tan around the tips. A sky-blue surface and lime green surround the midnight black pupils at the top tips. The beak is bright pink with a silver candy stone in the center. The breast of the flower is small and round with black furry dots all over. In between the head and breast, there are sleek black wings covered in white furry dots. At the point where the breast and the torso meet, there are snow white feathers that flare out and continue and cling to the bottom portion of the body. The lower body is a deep violet with snow-white feathers randomly appearing throughout the lower body.

Hansen chuckled softly as she rambled on. "My dear, you sound utterly enchanted."

"I *am* enchanted!" Crosby replied, her voice brimming with wonder. "And the grass smells like lavender, but sweeter… like it's been kissed by honey or something."

"The sweetness you smell," came a melodic voice from nowhere, "It is the pollen spreading throughout the kingdom. It's why the air feels so alive here," Hansen replied with a generous smile.

Crosby rubbed her eyes as she took in the gorgeous flowers. Hansen had a smirk on his face as he knew what was coming.

"Hansen!" Crosby exclaimed in excitement.

"I know, my dear; I am right here with you, and this is my world, after all," Hansen replied.

"Yes, but are you actually seeing what I am seeing?" Asked Crosby.

"Why don't you tell me what it is that you are so excited about, my dear," said Hansen

"You would think that I would be surprised by the fact that you are talking to me. I have concluded that everyone in this kingdom can speak, read minds, and have some form of magical power," said Crosby.

"Well then, I hope that you enjoy your stroll through this area," replied Hansen.

Hansen smirked, clearly unbothered. "You've met another of my friends."

The voice chuckled softly, and Crosby's gaze landed on one of the bat-like flowers swaying gently. Its golden diamond glimmered as it spoke again. "You'd think my ability to talk would surprise you, child. But from what I've heard, you've already learned that this kingdom is filled with magic and wonder."

Crosby blinked rapidly, her voice rising in pitch. "Wait! Are you not my next encounter? Am I not supposed to learn something from you, and what is your name?"

The flower chuckled again, "Darling, you are simply walking through here as you will be meeting the High Commander now." My beautiful friend, my name is Lindee."

"Oh, my goodness, Hansen!" Crosby breathed, turning to Hansen, "The one time I don't ask about the High Commander is the time that I am going to meet him."

Hansen chuckled, the sound deep and soothing, "Sometimes, Crosby, when we get focused on the things that matter and are important, we receive a blessing. As you recall, you had somewhat of a puzzle to untangle; you and Rehn worked through the puzzling factor in your journey."

Crosby took a deep breath, her voice still tinged with nervousness, and because of the risk of sounding redundant, "Hansen... is it *really* time? Am I ready?"

Hansen's tone softened, "Not quite yet, Crosby; this is the part where you will enjoy the land and continue to search your heart. This is important because it will help you to be prepared for the High Commander."

Crosby hesitated before asking, her voice quiet, "Hansen, may I ask you a question?"

"Of course, you can, dear," he replied, his expression kind, "Remember, I'm here for whatever need you might have during your journey through my Kingdom."

"When you say I need to prepare myself for meeting the High Commander," she asked slowly, "Is there any reason for me to be afraid?"

Hansen tilted his head, his eyes softening, "My dear, why on earth would you think that there would be any reason for you to experience any fear?"

Crosby shuffled her feet, looking down, "Well, usually in my world, when someone says for them to prepare themselves, it is most often bad news or a horrible experience."

"Oh dear, I'm truly sorry about that." Hansen said, his voice gentle and reassuring, "That is not the case in my Kingdom. I am just asking you to prepare for the grandeur that you will meet. You must understand that meeting the High Commander is a great privilege."

Crosby let out a small, relieved sigh, her shoulders relaxing. "Okay, that makes me feel a little better. I guess I'll try to prepare, then."

Hansen smiled, his voice warm. "That's all I ask, my dear. Let the beauty of this land guide you, and you'll be ready when the time comes."

Chapter Twenty-Eight

Why me?

As they continued along the pathway toward the High Commander, Crosby began to review every conversation and person she had encountered on this journey. She thought about the drawing that she had put on the chalkboard and suddenly came to a startling realization that it was because of her drawing that she had entered the Magical Kingdom.

How could I not have known this before? she wondered, her thoughts racing in her little mind. As she mentally visualized the classroom, she remembered how Ms. Traci seemed really excited when she first placed her hand on the exquisite doorknob. Her mind is now racing at the many possibilities and circumstances for her to be chosen to experience such a wonderful journey. She now knows without a shadow of a doubt that she has just received the answer to the *"Why Me"* question she had at the beginning of her journey. Yet another question emerged: How does Ms. Traci fit into all of this?

"I'm very proud of the deduction that you have come to, Crosby," Hansen said with a warm smile, his voice filled with admiration, "I knew that you would eventually have your *aha* moment. Of course, I do realize that your mind is still buzzing with questions. I also know that you still need more quiet time to continue to mull over everything that you have experienced. But please remember, I'm here for you. That said, this is the point where you take charge of how we proceed toward the High Commander. Please note that you will meet the High Commander, but your experience will depend entirely on how you take the knowledge my friends have shared with you.

Crosby fell into an even deeper concentration after receiving these words from Hansen. She knew that she could easily just ask Hansen to explain everything throughout her journey, but she also sensed that Hansen wouldn't make it that easy. He knows this is too important to let me skip through the experience, she thought. Amid all these things running through her mind, she was more focused and was still questioning the role that Ms. Traci had been playing in this experience. She was bound and determined to figure this part out on her own.

In her mind, she places herself in the middle of the classroom to examine everything that surrounds her. She slowly rotates her body in a circular motion to grasp everything on the walls and floor. "Hansen," she said suddenly, her voice tinged with urgency, "May I please look into your eyes? I need to see something more clearly in my classroom."

Hansen's expression softened with understanding as he knelt and lowered his face to her level for her to look into his eyes and find what she was searching for at this moment. "Of course, Crosby," he said gently. "Take your time."

As Crosby gazed deeply into Hansen's eyes, her mind sharpened; immediately, she focused on the different textures and details on the walls. She saw the wall adorned with emojis, where students placed stickers to express their emotions.

The beautiful serenity wall with bean bags on the floor and stickers stating, *"Wish I was here,"* and the famous chalkboard wall with different drawings from different students. At that moment, she noticed something she had missed! Her drawing is wrapped in a large heart with the tiniest smiley face at the bottom right-hand side of the heart. She hadn't drawn that.

Her eyes widened as she spotted another detail: on the slate of her antique desk, where her name had always been written, the bold letters now read, *"Crosby's Journey begins today."* She shifted her focus to Ms. Traci, who was lovingly staring at the beautiful door that Crosby crossed what felt like ages ago.

"Hansen," Crosby said, her voice brimming with revelation, "Is Ms. Traci a part of your kingdom? I know that it is because of her and my drawing that I was chosen. I know because I am not the one who encircled my drawing with a large heart and a smiley emoji at the bottom. Her classroom is unique to all the other classrooms in my school. I always just thought that it was because she is so caring and emotionally invested in her students. This makes me wonder if there have been other students who have experienced a journey such as this before me. She has been a teacher in our school for over three years. There is no way that someone else hasn't made this journey."

Hansen's eyes twinkled with approval. "Yes, Crosby, you are absolutely correct," he said warmly. "Ms. Traci is a part of my kingdom. Her compassion and love for her students are the reason that we approached her many years ago when she first began teaching. She has never herself entered my kingdom as there has never been the need for her to visit. She understands the importance of keeping my kingdom safe for all who experience this wonderful and clarifying journey. When we approached her, she was full of questions for us. She wanted to make sure that our goal was simply for the betterment of her students. None of her colleagues and supervisors are aware of her involvement with my kingdom. Every person who has entered my kingdom never remembers entering through the magical door. As I told you before, your recollection will simply be that of a very detailed dream you have experienced."

Crosby's heart swelled with understanding as the pieces finally started to come together. She looked up at Hansen, her resolve strengthening. This journey was hers to embrace—and she was ready for whatever lay ahead.

Chapter Twenty-Nine

Recollecting the Advice

Now that Crosby has a clearer understanding of why she has been chosen, she decides that it is time to focus on how to proceed in her journey to make the changes needed for her and her family's future. She knows that this is the portion of her journey that will tug at her heart the most. Her family's happiness is extremely important to her, and she will make sure to accept everything full-heartedly.

Lost in thought, she is startled by Hansen's gentle voice. "Crosby," he says warmly, "I believe that you have matured so much through this journey that I am confident in saying that you will make smart choices where you and your family are concerned."

Crosby's face lights up with a glorious smile, her heart swelling with gratitude. "Thank you, Hansen," she replies softly, her voice brimming with emotion. "That means so much to me. I hope I can live up to that trust."

As Crosby and Hansen continue through the gorgeous Bat Valley, as she has decided to name it. She is thinking about how Sedro had expressed that she would get clarification on her situation as soon as she was ready to receive her truths.

Hansen's earlier comment about her maturity now feels even more significant. She realizes she's grown in ways she never expected.

"It wasn't me who started the division in my family," she thinks, "but I did make it worse. My actions toward the adults in my family weren't always the best. I wasn't the only one who made mistakes, but I can't control anyone else's choices, only my own."

Crosby takes a deep breath as the realization washes over her. She knows what needs to change. She realizes that having her father in her life and the man who makes her mother happy can coexist without all the drama. She understands that treating her mother's boyfriend, Jason, with such disregard hurt her mother more than she can imagine. She feels that her mother lashing out at her father was simply because she didn't know how to handle Crosby's disrespect towards her.

"I can do better," Crosby resolves silently. "I can embrace the changes in our family and help my sister do the same. It won't happen overnight, but I can take the first step." However, she will make these changes. She is aware that everything in life takes time to mend.

As she is walking, she hears a delicate voice. This is the first time she hears one of the flower bats speak. "Crosby, what a delight to know that as you journeyed through our kingdom, you didn't just enjoy the land. I am fully impressed by the fact that as young as you are, you took the time to receive the advice that was carefully given to you by our friends."

Crosby's eyes widen in amazement. "Oh! I... I am sorry," she stammers, blushing slightly. "I truly don't know how to address you as I don't know your name."

The flower bat chuckles softly, her wings shimmering as she dips in the air. "Oh, my dear, I'm so very sorry. My name is Lyndee, and I am pleased to meet you."

Crosby smiles warmly. "Well, Lyndee, it is my pleasure indeed to make your acquaintance."

Lyndee and Crosby continued in their conversation as Hansen listened intently and pondered over the discussion. There is something in the discussion that is sending happy, bubbly feelings through Hansen's body as they speak. Hansen notices that Crosby has accepted Jason as part of the family. She doesn't even know it yet.

Hansen decides to let her make this connection on her own. He knows that once she recognizes this truth, she'll feel the sense of warmth and peace she's been longing for. Smiling to himself, he watches as Crosby and Lyndee continue to talk, her laughter mingling with the soft rustle of the valley breeze.

She's ready, he thinks. She's truly ready to meet the High
Commander.

115

Chapter Thirty

Apparent Change

Although Hansen is practically giddy with excitement, Crosby remains blissfully unaware, completely entranced with Lyndee and her fellow bat plants fluttering around her. When Crosby entered the kingdom, she was so disillusioned by her family's discord that she couldn't seem to find anything positive to hold onto but walking through this journey, she has been able to find peace within her heart.

As they all listen to Crosby speak of her wonderful family, since they are in a magical kingdom, they are all aware of the change in Crosby's disposition concerning her family. The flower bats, Lyndee included, can feel the change in her disposition. The excitement in the land is glorious and cheerful. Crosby believes it is because of her storytelling and her experiences in the journey. With a bright smile, she continues to share her antidotes and special elaborations on the history of her family with a newfound affection.

She pauses as she recalls one particular moment where Jason is cooking dinner for everyone. "Oh, he was dancing in the kitchen!" she exclaims with a soft laugh. "We were all sitting at the table, just watching him, laughing so hard. He wasn't embarrassed in the slightest!" Her face lights up with the warmth of the memory, but then her eyes widen suddenly, and her expression freezes in surprise. Everyone around her watches and smiles as they gently guide her through her realization.

"Hansen!" Crosby blurts out, her voice brimming with astonishment. "Do you realize what just happened? I am okay with my entire family! I am not feeling any anger nor disgruntled feelings towards my mother or Jason."

Hansen's eyes soften with pride, and he nods. "I do realize that, my dear. You have made progress through this journey. I am so very proud of you, Crosby."

Crosby grins, her cheeks flushing slightly. "Hansen, this may sound bad, but I am proud of myself, too."

Hansen's tone turns firm but kind. "There is no reason for you to feel bad about something so positive. Many times, people are afraid to honor their accomplishments for fear of feeling selfish. It is very important that you not feel this way; this can, at times, erase all your progress simply because you allow yourself to be ashamed of celebrating your accomplishments."

Lyndee, unable to contain her delight, bursts into joyful laughter, sending a wave of happiness to all her other friends.

Their wings shimmer in the light, and Crosby feels their shared joy radiating through her.

Overcome with excitement, Crosby decided to share in the joy and excitement and began to happily run through the garden of flower bats. The moment was so joyous that their laughter continued. Crosby decided that at this very moment, she felt the most stress-free she had felt in years.

As Crosby was running through the garden, Lyndee decided to address Hansen, her voice soft and knowing. "Hansen, it looks like the search for her missing piece has reached its end. I do believe that Crosby has regained that which was lost so long ago."

Hansen nods, his eyes gleaming. "I was just thinking the same thing, Lyndee. It truly is a glorious moment, one that will linger in her heart forever. This is a glorious affair, to say the least. Do you agree with me, Lyndee?"

"Hansen, I do believe that we are both on the same page in this matter," Lyndee replies with a satisfied smile, lifting her wings high into the air. Instantly, the flower bats fall silent.

Lyndee simply raised her wings as high as they could reach, and every flower bat went silent immediately. "Crosby," Lyndee calls gently, "I hear that you like to sing! I think that we should take this moment and celebrate it in song; what do you think?"

Crosby stops mid-run, her eyes wide with awe. "Wait, can we first address the fact that you are lifting your wings, and everything went silent is totally amazing! Second, of course, I want to celebrate with a song or twelve."

Hansen chuckles, shaking his head. "Now, Crosby, let's not get too crazy with the number of songs we shall sing."

"Really, Hansen?" Lyndee interjects, her tone playful but firm. "Hansen, please quit sucking all the joy out of this child; Rehn told me how you wouldn't enjoy the fun land with her! Now let's just sing, worry about how many songs we sing when the time gets to the point that we must move forward."

Hansen groans, rolling his eyes dramatically. "You and Rehn need to let it go! I never chose to be this large, I can't help the fact that I am too large to enjoy the fun land. I say we should just sing, Crosby; what song should we start with?"

Before Crosby can answer, she hesitates. "Hansen, before we move forward with all of this excitement, may I please look into your eyes and check in on my family?"

Without hesitation, Hansen lowers himself to her level, his gaze steady and kind. As Crosby peers into his eyes, the world around her shifts, and she begins to see her family.

The first person she saw was her little sister, Hailey, was on the playground sitting all by herself, looking sad; this hurt Crosby to her core. "Oh, Hailey," she thinks, tears stinging her eyes. "I can't fix this for you, but I'll be there for you. We'll both need help to heal." She knows that she can't be the one to help her sister. Hailey will have to go to counseling to make the changes needed for her to be happy again. This is something that they will both need.

Next, she saw her father. Even though there is sadness in his eyes, he seems to be enjoying his lunch with a woman she has never seen. She isn't sure how this woman fits into her father's life. "He looks... happy," she realizes.

She decided it was time to look in on her mother. As she watched her mother with Jason, she realized that she hadn't seen her mother this happy in a very long time. The realization hits her like a wave: "Mom hasn't been this happy because I wouldn't let myself see it. My anger blinded me to everything else." She feels as though her actions contributed to the sadness they were all feeling.

As the visions fade, Crosby settles herself and her own thoughts for a moment. "Their love for us hasn't changed," she thinks. "Just because they're not together anymore doesn't mean they love us any less. Couples drift apart—it happens—but they're both finding happiness in their own ways."

A smile breaks across Crosby's face, one that lights up her entire being. It's the kind of smile that reaches her eyes and warms her heart. She can see that her mother is happy and that her father is moving on as well and is trying to find his own happiness. Crosby is ready to embrace her new family and begin to make new, wonderful memories with them. She realizes that while on this journey, as she took in all the advice she was given, she learned to accept the changes that are happening in her family. She is ready to truly be a part of her growing family and look at it as a positive change rather than a disaster.

As Crosby reflects on her journey, she is reminded of the knowledge she has received. Hansen taught her that it is okay to embrace your fears and accomplishments. Sedro taught her that even though she may know the surface of a problem, sometimes we must wait until her heart is ready to accept the harsh truth. Tailey taught that it is okay to express and own your feelings. She knows that she has to be sure not to allow her feelings to engulf her. Rehn helped her to see that she only has control of her actions, and that she is solely responsible for her actions.

With a deep breath and renewed hope, Crosby steps forward, ready to embrace her future.

Chapter Thirty-One

Singing with Flower Bats

Crosby turns to Lyndee with a grin as wide as the horizon. "I want us to sing a happy song!" she exclaims, her excitement radiating like sunlight through the magical land.

"Perfect!" Lyndee responds, her voice lilting with joy.

They all stop and take a moment to think about a song that will be happy and fitting. Crosby furrows her brow in concentration but suddenly lets out a shriek and yells, "I know what song we can sing!!" she shouts, her enthusiasm bubbling over. Everyone burst into laughter at the sight of Crosby's excitement. She overlooks the fact that everyone is laughing and announces the song that she wants everyone to sing with her. Without any hesitation, everyone is delighted and begins to sing with Crosby.

If you're happy and you know it, clap your hands,

If you're happy and you know it, clap your hands,

If you're happy and you know it, then your life will surely know.

If you're happy and you know it, clap your hands.

They went on to sing about stomping their feet, winking their eyes, turning around, and shouting for joy. Each verse brought laughter, their voices blending into a harmonious celebration of happiness.

The group continued to sing more songs as they traveled through the land. They sang songs like My Happy Song, This is My Happy Face, and wildly energetic Pop the Bubbles. The songs were so fun and delightful that time seemed to just get away from them.

After a moment, Lyndee realized how long they had been singing. She chose this time to inform Hansen that they probably needed to wrap things up. She raised her wings in a gentle signal. "Hansen," she murmured, her voice just loud enough to catch his attention, "I think it's time we start wrapping things up." When the announcement was made that they needed to wrap things up, Crosby and the flower bats all began to feel sad.

Hansen nodded solemnly, and with a deep breath, he addressed the group, "Friends," he began, his voice kind but firm, "There is no reason for this sadness. We simply need to move forward so that Crosby can conclude her journey and get back to her family."

A soft wave of melancholy swept over Crosby and the flower bats. Their wings drooped slightly, and the joyous atmosphere dimmed just a bit.

Hansen stepped forward, his tone soothing yet resolute. "This isn't goodbye forever. It's simply the next step. Crosby's journey has brought her so much growth and strength; her family needs her now more than ever."

Crosby nodded, wiping away a stray tear that had threatened to fall. She hugged Lyndee tightly, then waved farewell to the flower bats, who fluttered and chirped in an affectionate goodbye.

They make a silent decision that they will walk slowly rather than a rapid walk. Crosby is still allowing her thoughts to catch up to her reality. She knows that the changes that are coming are wonderful. However, she also knows that it will take time. She will have to allow everyone involved to understand and accept the changes. She is mostly thinking of her sister. Her parents will probably accept the changes quicker and be less reluctant.

Crosby believes that once she and the grown-ups sit down for a conversation about how to mend the family, they will be willing to make the changes necessary. Her thoughts lingered on Hailey. "She might surprise me," Crosby thought. "She's always hated seeing me upset. Maybe she'll be willing to try, just for me." She has always been that sister that wants to make everyone proud and happy. She knows that the first thing she wants to do when she sees her sister is wrap her arms around her for as long as she allows. A soft smile spread across her face as she imagined wrapping her sister in a warm hug and holding on for as long as Hailey would let her.

She pictured the grown-ups sitting down with her to discuss mending their fractured family. She felt a flicker of hope. "If we can talk honestly—if we're willing to make changes—I know we can find happiness again."

Hansen knew that this revelation that Crosby was having was important for her mental healing. He carefully watched and silently guided her as they continued to walk. He offered no words, silently guiding her with his steady presence, his heart swelling with pride at her progress. He knew that, eventually, she would wake from processing the situation her family was experiencing. Crosby needed this moment to reflect and accept.

Suddenly, Crosby looked up at Hansen with an expression on her face that was almost comical. He looked at her with admiration but couldn't help but chuckle.

Hansen tilted, "What is it, Crosby?" he asked, his voice soft and encouraging.

She didn't answer immediately, her gaze darting around. "Hansen," she finally whispered, her voice tinged with awe, "Have you noticed? The land... it's different somehow. It's... brighter."

Hansen followed her gaze, smiling knowingly. "Ah, Crosby," he said, "perhaps the land is simply reflecting you."

Chapter Thirty-Two

Experiencing the magic

Crosby felt like she was floating on air, her every step feather-light against the celestial terrain. The sense of a majestic aura had spread throughout the enchanted land. She glanced around in disbelief, marveling at the astonishing pearl-gray clouds stretched out before her. They had the essence of the fluffiest exotic material in existence. Their golden-tipped edges shimmered, giving the impression of delicate, otherworldly fabric, soft and impossibly luxurious. A soft and magical scent floated through the air, warm and comforting, like sweet amber that felt timeless. Crosby took a deep breath, enjoying the smell, and felt a calm and peaceful respect wash over her. It was as if the land asked for honor but in a kind and gentle way.

"Hansen," she said softly, her voice a mixture of awe and anticipation, "I get the distinct feeling that we are in the presence of The High Commander."

Hansen's expression grew serious, though his eyes glimmered with pride. "Crosby, your feelings are legitimately precise and are not failing you, as always," he replied. "You are exactly right. The moment has come for you to meet the High Commander, evaluate the advice you were given, and learn how to better apply it in your life. This will also be helpful as you will gain an understanding of how to instruct the adults in your life to manage a new way of life. When you return to your world, you will be able to live a life with less stress and more enjoyment."

Crosby nodded, her heart pounding with anticipation. She continued to be in awe of her surroundings. She sensed the distinction of supreme eminence flowing throughout the land. As she felt the palpitation of her heart hastened in her excitement, the grin she was wearing began to grow. Yet, beneath her excitement, there was a warm ember of joy growing steadily. Her grin stretched wider, unable to be contained.

She realized that not only was she extremely close to meeting the High Commander, but the moment also when she got to see her family again was quickly approaching. As much as she had thoroughly enjoyed herself with everyone in this amazing kingdom, she was ready to see her family and wrap her arms around her little sister.

As they continued walking, Crosby glanced at Hansen with a nostalgic smile. "You know," she began, her voice tinged with wistfulness, "these clouds remind me of marshmallows. They're just like the ones we roasted on our family camping trip."

She laughed softly, her gaze turning inward to the memory. "Dad surprised us with that trip. It wasn't really his thing—he's more of a 'hotel and room service' kind of guy. But he did it for Mom. He was still trying to make her happy back then."

Crosby was truly happy that she believed their family would be better when she returned to her world. Her voice wavered slightly, but she quickly steadied herself, determination shining in her eyes. "I really believe that things will be better when I go back. I can feel it."

Hansen, sensing her growing nervousness, offered a small smile and simply let her talk. He knew her rambling was a way of easing the tension, and he wanted her to process her thoughts fully before the monumental meeting ahead.

As they continued their journey, Crosby began to notice subtle changes in the clouds around them as they were strolling through the land. The pearl-gray clouds with the golden tips are more of a golden pearl and even more majestic than earlier, and the light intensifies with every step. The wonderful scent in the land was getting even sweeter than it already was if that was even possible. The excitement Crosby was feeling intensified, knowing that she was even closer now. There was no doubt in her mind what this change in the atmosphere meant.

"Hansen," she said quietly, her voice brimming with excitement, "the clouds... they're changing again."

Hansen chuckled, his tone light but knowing. "You're observant, Crosby. The land always reflects what's near."

Her heart raced as her surroundings became even more breathtaking. She was certain now—this transformation in the atmosphere could only mean one thing. The High Commander was nearby.

Chapter Thirty-Three

The Time has Come

Crosby's eyes brightened, and her smile widened. The High Commander was the most beautiful woman she had ever seen. Her skin was silky shimmering porcelain, her eyes a greenish-gray color with a hint of lavender speckles around the pupils. Her long golden hair has minimal light brown streaks encompassing her face.

The High Commander wore a flowing white dress with shimmering lace sleeves that hugged her arms. The waistline was fitted, and the skirt puffed out slightly, moving gracefully as she stood. There were tiny gold hearts at the neckline that gently swooped just below her throat and at the bottom of the skirt. As her body moves, her hearts are caught by the sun, so the shimmer sends starbursts into the clouds.

Crosby was completely captivated by the radiant beauty and grace of the High Commander.

"Hello, my sweet girl," the High Commander greeted, her voice soft and kind. "I'm so glad to see that you have made it through my Kingdom. I am truly impressed by your level of maturity."

Crosby's eyes brighten, "Hello, your Highness, it is my pleasure to finally meet you."

The High Commander's gentle smile widened. "Oh dear, thank you so much for your reverence towards me. Since we will be getting to know each other better, why don't you call me Amina."

Crosby's eyes lit up, "Oh my, that is such a beautiful name. I want you to know that your Kingdom has been a wonderful experience for me, and everyone I have met has been exceptionally kind to me."

Amina's face softened with affection. "That's wonderful, my dear Crosby. How about we get to know each other? I want you to know that I have kept a close eye on you through Hansen. The struggles you have endured have been more than a child should ever have to handle. Sometimes, adults choose to confide in their children more than they should during a family split, or they unconsciously blame them for the turmoil they are experiencing. I dare to say that you have experience being blamed for things that can't possibly be your doing."

"But I am grateful for Ms. Traci for watching out for you wonderful children and willing to act for your betterment." The High Commander continued in the same soft tone.

Crosby nodded, her heart swelling with gratitude for Ms. Traci's presence in her life.

Amina continued, her voice kind but steady. "You are aware that you are here because of your drawing on the chalkboard? I wonder if you know what it was that you lost in the process of your parents' divorce? I am hopeful that everyone you encountered here in my kingdom was an asset to the healing process you experienced. Do you believe that you are fully prepared to journey back to your world? Now that you have allowed me to set out the questions that will need to be addressed by us, I say that we begin to answer them one at a time."

Crosby straightened up, determination shining in her eyes. "Yes, I understand now that my drawing is what brought me here."

Amina tilted her head slightly. "Let's start with my first question, shall we?"

"Yes," Crosby said, nodding earnestly.

"Are you aware that the drawing is what brought you to us?" the High Commander asked.

"Yes," Crosby nodded her head again. "While I was on my journey, we met Sedro. Sedro let me know that it was, in fact, the drawing and its meaning that brought me here."

"So, you explored the meaning of drawing with Hansen and Sedro?" Amina smiled while asking the question.

"Yes, there were things that Sedro told me I would not understand until I was ready. At first, I didn't understand, and it made me a little angry, but then I realized through the help of Rehn that sometimes we must prepare our minds to accept the more difficult things in our lives."

Amina smiled, pride glowing in her expression. "How fortunate you are to have such an intellectual mind at your age... How wise you've become, Crosby."

Chapter Thirty-Four

Revealing the growth

"Crosby, do you know what it was that you lost during your parents' divorce?" Amina asked gently, her kind eyes resting on Crosby.

Crosby nodded, her voice steady but soft. "Yes, Amina, I do know what I lost during my parents' divorce. At first, I couldn't understand how one can lose their smile, but while speaking with Bailey, she helped me to understand. I wasn't aware of the fact that a smile stems from your heart, and because it does people can feel the warmth you are sharing with them. Bailey also helped me to see that even though I was still smiling at my friends and family, my smile was not reaching my eyes; therefore, the spark and warmth weren't present."

Amina's expression softened even more, her smile full of pride. "Crosby, this is a very important gift to understand and hold. This will help you to see this in other people's lives, you will be able to help some to understand. Please never take this for granted, nor expect it to be your duty to help everyone. Having this gift is for your happiness, not everyone around you. Remember that a smile is contagious, and this is the best way for you to utilize it. Making sure that your smile is always genuine is the only expectation required of you."

Crosby smiled warmly, her heart feeling lighter with Amina's words.

Amina continued, her tone filled with encouragement. "Now we come to the point where we find out if everything you learned here was helpful. Do you feel the tools and lessons provided by everyone you've met were enough?"

Oh, I have learned so much," Crosby replied eagerly. "From learning about my smile to knowing how to breathe correctly when I am feeling anxious. I also learned that it is not my responsibility to mend nor keep my family together; it is only my job to be a child and give my entire family my genuine love and affection."

Amina's eyes sparkled with pride. "Crosby, I am so very proud of you. I am excited to watch you grow and continue to embrace every life lesson full-heartedly."

Amina's voice softened. "Crosby, do you believe that you feel ready to return to your home?"

Crosby hesitated for a moment, her expression bittersweet. "Amina, I will be honest; it is going to be difficult to leave this glorious place, but I am truly ready to be home with my family."

"Very well then," Amina said gently. "I will prepare you for your departure from my world into yours."

Crosby's face brightened with a thought. "Amina, before we prepare for my departure, may I ask you a favor and a question?"

"Absolutely, my dear," Amina said warmly. "Ask me anything that your heart desires."

"Will I ever be able to return to your kingdom simply to visit all the friends I have made?" Crosby asked hopefully.

Amina's smile was soft but firm. "Crosby, I promise you that when you go home, your life will be different and wonderful. We will only be a fond dream sequence in your life."

Crosby's eyes welled with emotion. "Amina, that makes me feel sad and happy at the same time. Is that possible?"

Amina chuckled lightly. "Yes, my dear, because we will always be a happy thought in your mind."

Crosby took a deep breath and said, "When I met Sedro, I was able to sing with him. Bailey and I had a wonderful time together. Rehn built me an amusement park and Lyndee and all the flower bats sang songs with me. Hansen has become my best friend and knows everything about me and my family. Is it possible for me to have a proper goodbye from both of you?"

Amina tilted her head, curiosity in her eyes. "What is it that you wish for Hansen and I? Neither of us sings, and there isn't anything that I can build for you. We have conversed about you and your family; you have even shared your joy here in my kingdom with us."

Crosby smiled sweetly. "Oh, it's very simple, you see; all that I want from the both of you is a hug that can last me a lifetime."

Amina's smile widened, and Hansen, standing nearby, nodded warmly. "Well, my dear, that is a very easy request," Amina said.

They all gathered in a circle, taking turns giving each other heartfelt hugs. For some reason, none of them could get enough, holding on just a little longer each time as though they wanted to lock the warmth and love into their hearts forever.

Chapter Thirty-Five

Going Home

After what felt like many hours of heartfelt conversations and warm embraces, Amina steadied her voice, her tone calm yet full of emotions. "Crosby, the time has come for you to return your home," she said softly.

Crosby felt a wave of bittersweet sadness wash over her. "I'll miss you, Amina," she whispered, her voice trembling slightly.

Amina smiled warmly, her eyes shining with encouragement. "And we will always be with you, my dear, in your heart. Now, I want you to close your eyes; I will count with you backward from twenty. When you open your eyes, you will be back at your desk in your classroom. Please remember that you will always have Ms. Traci to lean on when you have a bad day. It will be up to you to reach out and ask for help; only then can she help you. You will also have your parents to help guide you. They love you more than you know."

Crosby nodded, her eyes fluttering closed as Amina began the countdown.

"Twenty... nineteen..." Amina's voice was steady and soothing, a gentle anchor.

Crosby joined in, her own voice trembling but growing steadier with each number. As they counted down, Amina's voice became faint, growing softer and softer until it was no more than a faded whisper.

When Crosby reached "one," she opened her eyes. She was back at her desk in her classroom, sunlight streaming through the window.

Ms. Traci was standing at Crosby's side when she opened her eyes. Even though she knew of the experience Crosby had had, she was surprised when Crosby got out of her chair and wrapped her arms around her waist.

"Thank you, Ms. Traci," Crosby whispered, her voice thick with emotion.

Ms. Traci, though surprised by the sudden hug, immediately returned the embrace. A warm smile spread across her face, and she felt a sense of certainty. At that moment, Ms. Traci knew that Crosby was going to be okay.

The bell for school dismissal rang, and all the children filed out of the classroom. Crosby stayed behind.

"I'm so sorry, Ms. Traci," Crosby said earnestly. "I didn't mean to fall asleep during class. But I had the most wonderful dream, and now I need to go see my family."

Ms. Traci chuckled softly, patting Crosby's shoulder. "It's alright, sweetheart. Go on, now."

Crosby ran out to the playground to find her sister at the place where they always met. When she saw her sister, she ran to her and embraced her so tightly that Hailey couldn't help but burst out in laughter.

"Crosby!" Hailey exclaimed, her laughter ringing out as she tried to catch her breath. "What's gotten into you?"

While they waited for their mother to pick them up, Crosby shared her dream with her sister, her words tumbling out in an excited rush. "I feel like it was a sign," Crosby said, her eyes shining with hope. "It's like everything's going to be okay. I just know it."

As their mother approached them from the parking lot, Crosby ran to her and hugged her tightly.

"Mom, I'm so sorry," Crosby said, her voice thick with emotion. "Can we all talk tonight? I need to say something to everyone—together."

Her mother, though surprised, nodded gently, brushing Crosby's hair back from her face. "Of course, sweetheart. We'll all be there."

Later that evening, after they had had dinner because Crosby had insisted that everyone had to be present, they all sat in the living room waiting for an explanation.

Taking a deep breath, Crosby began. "I need to ask for forgiveness," she said, her voice clear but filled with emotion. "I know I didn't cause the problems between all of you, but I've been carrying a lot of anger and sadness. I think it's been hurting all of us. I want us to be okay again. I want us to get along—for me and Hailey. We'll be so much happier if we can all just agree to try."

She let Jason know that even though he could never be her father, she would always have room for him in her heart.

The room was silent for a moment, but then, one by one, tears began to fall. Hugs were shared, and forgiveness was granted. The tension that had once filled the family seemed to dissolve in the warmth of the moment.

The rest of the evening was filled with laughter, happy tears, and promises to move forward together. Crosby felt a sense of peace settles over her. For the first time in a long time, she truly believed everything was going to be okay.

As she sat on the couch listening to a story her mother was sharing, she heard a distant, familiar voice say, "Success." Crosby's eyes widened in wonderment! "Where have I heard that voice before?"